DANGEROUS SPACES

Anthea murmured protestingly but did not wake. She slept, and in her sleep her left hand closed around her right wrist and felt the copper bracelet rising up out of her skin, coming through the skin, become real under her horrified fingertips. A voice spoke to her from nonexistent space. "I've got you now," Griff said triumphantly. "We're going on, and this time we won't stop until we get there."

"While there are other dreamworlds in other books, Mahy's . . . is unique in its slow slide from entrancing to spellbinding, its transformation from a place of beauty to one of menace and danger."
—*School Library Journal*, starred review

"Breathtaking adventure combined with honest and memorable insights into the workings of a family. . . . This novel will linger in the mind of the reader."
—*Publishers Weekly*

DANGEROUS

SPACES

by Margaret Mahy

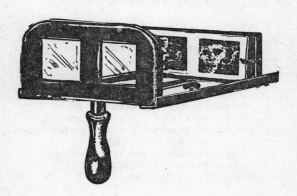

PUFFIN BOOKS

PUFFIN BOOKS

Published by the Penguin Group

Penguin Books USA Inc., 375 Hudson Street, New York, New York 10014, U.S.A.

Penguin Books Ltd, 27 Wrights Lane, London W8 5TZ, England

Penguin Books Australia Ltd, Ringwood, Victoria, Australia

Penguin Books Canada Ltd, 10 Alcorn Avenue, Toronto, Ontario, Canada M4V 3B2

Penguin Books (N.Z.) Ltd, 182–190 Wairau Road, Auckland 10, New Zealand

Penguin Books Ltd, Registered Offices: Harmondsworth, Middlesex, England

First published in the United States of America by Viking Penguin,
a division of Penguin Books USA Inc., 1991
Published in Puffin Books, 1993

1 3 5 7 9 10 8 6 4 2

LIBRARY OF CONGRESS CATALOGING-IN-PUBLICATION DATA

Mahy, Margaret.

Dangerous spaces / by Margaret Mahy. p. cm.

Summary: Two cousins living in a house that is haunted are drawn
at night into a dream world which threatens to overwhelm their real world.

ISBN 0-14-036362-9

[1. Cousins—Fiction.   2. Haunted houses—Fiction.
3. Supernatural—Fiction.   4. Space and time—Fiction.]   I. Title.

PZ7.M2773Dan   1993   [Fic]—dc20   92-44008   CIP   AC

Printed in the United States of America

To Cathy and Ron . . .

friends, librarians

astronomers and readers

Chapter 1

"I HAD THIS DREAM," said Anthea at breakfast. "I was in a high place climbing out of a crack in the world, and there was a hot wind blowing on me."

"You should have jumped," exclaimed Flora, "and floated . . . "

She flung out her arms to show how poetically *she* would have floated if it had been her dream.

"It wasn't that sort of dream," protested Anthea, tugging restlessly at the silver chain around her neck. "It was *real* . . . "

She wanted to explain how the crack had seemed to be closing *in* on her and opening *out* of her at the same time, but what words are there to describe a thing like that? Anthea sighed. She did not want anyone joking about her dream, yet it was the sort of dream that had to be told.

"*I* fly in dreams," Flora said, watching Anthea narrowly across the table. She waved her arms as she spoke, swaying right, swaying left . . . the beautiful swan girl. But then, catching sight of her reflection in the side of the new toaster that had fizzed and stopped going yesterday she suddenly fell silent. Never in a million years would she ever be a swan. Stiffening her arms she made the sound of an airplane instead . . . an airplane blotched with wartime camouflage.

Anthea's straight hair was the color of raw silk, and shone like silk, falling over her shoulders and down her back. The silver chain had a tiny silver padlock on it. She and Flora were both eleven, nearly twins, but Flora felt they looked as if they came from different planets.

"I don't fly! Just fall," Anthea said in a flat voice, and looked down into her plate of stewed apple. Flora cheered up. She might be as wide as a door and covered in freckles but at least she could hope to fly, one way or another. Still making the airplane noise, she went into a thirty-degree turn.

The bead curtain that hung across the kitchen doorway rattled like bones. Flora's mother Molly, barging out of the kitchen, walked straight into one of the airplane's wings. Milk splashed out of the jug she was carrying.

"Flora!" she cried despairingly. "How dare you spread out so far at this hour in the morning!"

"Pussy, pussy!" called Flora's little brother, Teddy, walking out through the bead curtain with nothing on but his vest. He had stepped out of his nappy in the kitchen. Flora could see it in between the beads, with the shape of his bottom still pressed into it. Teddy, interested in the little pool of spilled milk, squatted down beside it, trying to make Anthea's cat, Glorious, take an interest, too. He liked seeing cats lap, and sometimes tried to lap himself. Glorious, who was watching the morning rush from a comfortable stool, just twitched her whiskers contemptuously and pushed her curled-up front paws further under her pure white chest. She had come to live with the Wakefields as a part of Anthea's luggage, but she made herself at home far more quickly than Anthea had. It was Flora's cat, Taffeta, who had moved out into the orchard, slinking in furtively to gobble food . . . then rushing out again . . . behaving like an unwelcome stranger although she had lived in the old house all her life.

"This milk's supposed to go on your stewed apple, not the floor," said Molly, putting the jug down on the table.

"We're eating *naked* stewed apple!" said Flora, and Anthea laughed. Flora looked surprised, and then grinned, too. It was not often they were amused by the same things.

"Eat it any way you like," Molly said, whisking back through the bead curtain.

"Go on about your dream," Flora said loudly, partly so that Molly would hear her being nice to an orphan cousin, but partly because Anthea, even though she was sitting at breakfast with her eyes open and laughing at the thought of naked stewed apple, looked as if, in the deepest part of her mind, she were still dreaming. Flora wanted her to wake up and be ordinary.

"A crack in the world—and wind blowing up through it, never stopping . . . blowing all hard and dry . . . as if someone had just *ironed* it," Anthea said. A faint shiver crept up the back of Flora's neck as she, too, felt the ironed breath of the wind blowing endlessly out of a crack in the world. However, she was determined not to be too impressed by any dream of Anthea's.

"I had to climb up," Anthea went on. "Someone was calling . . . no, not calling exactly . . . just waiting. Anyhow, I had to find them."

"Who was it?" asked Flora.

"I thought it might be my mother or father," Anthea said wistfully. "I thought they might have got stuck at the top of the crack."

Anthea's parents had gone out sailing six months earlier, and had never come back. The yacht had been found, capsized, but the crew had vanished into the sea forever. Anthea, complete with her fluffy tortoiseshell cat, pretty dresses, silver chain, and raw silk hair, had come to live with Flora's family in the old family house their grandfather had built.

Now, Flora was supposed to like her every day instead of just once a year at Christmas, for she had become like a slightly older sister without actually being one.

But it is sometimes hard to like people simply because they are related to you . . . particularly very pretty people who you are also forced to feel sorry for. Beauty and spectacular bad luck make them glamorous, and it is hard to have a glamorous star living with you when you are round and solid and freckled, with short brown hair. Everyone fussed over Anthea hoping to make up for the terrible things that had happened to her. Nobody pestered *her* to mix mash for the hens or carry out the pig bucket, and Molly ironed Anthea's nightdress instead of letting her wear it crumpled. Flora desperately wanted Anthea to get over her bad luck, and then go and stay somewhere else. She felt there wasn't really room in the old house for both of them.

"Was it them? In the dream, I mean?" she asked. She couldn't help wanting to know.

But before Anthea could answer, Flora's father, Lionel, came storming into the room. He had been down the long drive, lined with old walnut trees, to get the morning paper which was thrown off a van that went by their house before it was properly light. Lionel had had to search for it in the long grass and weeds that grew around their gatepost, and he had grass seeds and biddibids stuck around the cuffs of his good going-to-the-office trousers. Lionel never reminded Anthea of his brother, her dead father, but somehow of Tigger in the Winnie-the-Pooh stories, perhaps because he was so bouncy and so ready to try anything for breakfast. Even his graying hair, bushy at the sides but thin on top, somehow managed to bounce.

"How are my girls!" he said. "Molly—that baby's lost his nappy again. His bum'll freeze!"

Molly came out of the kitchen with a bowl of stewed apple. She thrust it at him as if she were passing a football.

"For you, oh lord and master," she said sarcastically, and then scooped Teddy up under one arm as if he were a load of washing. He screamed with pleasure and alarm and waved his bare legs.

"What about toast?" Lionel asked greedily.

"The bread's cut. Use the toaster in the kitchen!" Molly said. "That one there fused yesterday. Old Lionel again! How did a nice boy like you ever come to have a father who goes around fusing toasters when he should be busy pushing up roses?"

"Oh well, you've got to expect that sort of thing, living in a haunted house," said Lionel cheerfully.

It was a family joke that the house was haunted by the ghost of his father, old Lionel, who had grown up in this house when it was only two rooms and an outside lavatory. He had loved it dearly. Now his descendant, young Lionel, dived into the kitchen, making the bead curtain chatter crossly to itself behind him.

Anthea saw Flora look uncomfortably around the room at the mention of ghosts, and she looked, too—just in case. There were no ghosts. All that haunted the room was the usual disorder.

The living room and the dining room had once been separate, but young Lionel had knocked out a wall to turn them into one space, and had stripped off the old lining so that the plumbing could be improved, the pipes relagged and new electrical wiring installed. Because he had never finished the work he had started (there had been a pile of smooth tongue-grooved boarding covered over with green plastic at one end of the room ever since Anthea had come there six months ago), living in Flora's house was like living inside a sort of skeleton, skin gone, and bones, nerves, and blood vessels revealed. Even the bedrooms weren't private in the way Anthea had once been used to, for there was a hole in the wall between her room and Flora's. The first thing she saw every morning was Flora's freckled face peering through the hole at her, peering but not smiling.

"There are no ghosts," Anthea said.

"Who said there were?" Flora asked rather aggressively. She raised her voice and shouted, "Anthea's telling me about her dream. Someone was *waiting* beside a crack in the world."

"Probably trying to buy stamps," Lionel called back. "I had to wait for ages yesterday."

The bead curtain was still swaying, like a storm of brown rain and black hailstones, but Flora caught a glimpse of him trying to shake the morning paper open with one hand, while firmly pushing bread down into the old toaster with the other. "What's the weather going to be like?"

"Fine! Fine! Fine!" called Molly gloomily, rushing through the big room and vanishing into the hall as she spoke. They desperately needed rain to fill their rainwater tanks.

Anthea leaned toward Flora.

"I climbed up," she murmured, speaking quickly, eager by now to get her story over and done with. "I got hold of the grass and squeezed out over the edge. I scratched my arms and thought my ribs would break. But I got there and lay on the snow . . . "

"Snow?" Flora shook her head incredulously. "Snow in summer?"

"It wasn't summer in the dream. Anyhow, I think it was too high up to have seasons . . . "

"Was it *them?*" asked Flora, meaning was it Anthea's vanished parents. By now she really wanted to know.

"No. It was a boy with sandy hair, really handsome . . . "

"Whoo-oo!" hooted Flora.

"No . . . younger than us. He looked a bit like Teddy, but he had bright blue eyes," Anthea said. "And he was carrying a box covered with green material . . . green with white flowers. He held it out to me and said, 'To the island!' And then I woke up."

"Safe in bed," said Flora, anxious to remind Anthea that she was just an ordinary girl and not someone magical having visions.

"In bed. Not safe!" Anthea answered. "You're not safe just because you're lying down."

"It's what they say . . . safe in bed," argued Flora.

"*They* don't know what they're talking about," Anthea replied. "It's just as dangerous there as anywhere else."

"Was he telling you to *go* to some island?" asked Flora.

Anthea looked uncertain. "I don't know," she said at last. "It sort of made sense in the dream but now it doesn't."

She put out her hand to the milk jug. As she did this Flora saw that the inner skin of her cousin's arms was printed with a scarlet pattern, a network of scrapes and scratches as if she really had been squeezing herself out of a crack in the world, struggling upward over a sharp edge into a cold space while everyone else slept peacefully in the late summer dark of the old house.

Chapter 2

ANTHEA THOUGHT she would never get used to mornings in Flora's house. It was like watching one of those old movies in which people rush jerkily backward and forward, rolling their eyes, flinging out their arms, and falling over things. Of course, films like those are silent, and Flora's house was always noisy with questions and answers, accusations, apologies, greetings, and farewells. But there was the same feeling of everyone moving frantically, banging into one another. People ate toast as they ran from room to room, looking for car keys or last night's homework. Doors slammed so loudly that the naked walls with their red and green and white electric wiring cracked and muttered in reply.

The strange thing was that, though Anthea felt she was watching an old film full of twitching shadows, she also felt that *she* was more of a shadow than anyone else, squashed by all the energy around her into a paper doll with a polite smile. Having been an only child in a house where mornings had hummed gently along and the people knew where things were because they had carefully put them ready the night before, there were times when Anthea felt she must somehow find a space where she could relax and breathe, or else remain a paper doll for the rest of her life. She did not want to argue like Flora, or shout like Molly. Once she started shouting, she knew she would never stop. She would shout and shout and shout, over and over again, until there was nothing left of her but an echo, weeping and then fading forever.

At home, the table had always been laid; pieces of toast had stood neatly in a flowery china toast-rack waiting to be chosen, and the honey had been in a silver pot with a silver bee on the lid. Now, that silver honey-pot, wrapped carefully in tissue paper, was packed away in a wooden chest, waiting for the day when Anthea had a home of her own once more.

"We'll keep it safely until then," Molly told her. "We're too rough for nice things around there."

Anthea had been happy to hide her treasures from Flora. She had been annoyed to see her cousin looking at them possessively, obviously thinking they ought to be shared. If Anthea could have wrapped herself in tissue paper and packed herself away with the honey-pot, she would have done so happily. Then, when things became better, when there was a true space for her, she would rise up out of the tissue paper (while people exclaimed at her beauty and value) and move gracefully into that space, where she would sit, looking serenely at the world.

Outside, there were wide hills around a wrinkling harbor full of their broken reflection. There was also a little tussocky peninsula where cattle grazed, and an island shaped like an ancient dragon dreaming under a clear sky. There was plenty of space out there. But between the house and the harbor lay the verandah, and when she glanced through the glass doors, she saw the verandah was already crowded. The Labrador bitch, Zeppelin, expecting puppies any day, ten hens, and a rooster, were all staring through the glass—anxious to get in and be part of the breakfast fun. Anthea loved Zeppelin, but the rooster was fierce. She was not as brave as Flora who had once thrown a bucket of water over him when he ruffled up his feathers and made for her bare legs.

"I'll just go . . ." Anthea began vaguely, not saying where she was going because she didn't quite know. She heard Flora sigh meaningfully as she drifted out, but she still pretended to drift, shutting the door firmly behind her. Then she leaned against it and let out a breath which she did not realize she had been holding. The dim hall ahead of her was the hollow spine of the house linking the big room to the old front door. It was a tidy spine, for the hall had been allowed to keep its original paneling, and had been carpeted in plain moss green. Molly polished the old brass handles on the bedroom doors opening off it, so that in some ways it seemed to be the most finished part of the house. And it was beautifully empty.

Almost empty. The long portrait of old Lionel, Lionel's father and the father of Anthea's own father, was watching her. Wherever you stood in the hall, old Lionel's painted eyes followed you. That's how you could tell the picture was true art, or so Flora had declared. Old Lionel had grown up in part of this house, had wandered over the hills and on to the peninsula, and had rowed in an old boat out to the island. His little brother, dead Henry, had lain for two days in the front room, contained by a small oak coffin with polished brass handles. His sister Anne had been married in springtime, out in the blossoming orchard of knobbly apple trees. Years later, after he had finished working in the city as a doctor, old Lionel had come back to the house and had saved it, extending the roof, adding the verandah, and building on the very kitchen, living room, and laundry which young Lionel had begun to change around.

Old Lionel, however, had hated all changes except his own, had hated the new plantations of pines, advancing in long straight lines over the bare hills around the harbor; he had hated the new houses along the road to the city, and the new people, new cars, and new dogs who lived in them. "What fifty people can enjoy, five hundred people will destroy," old Lionel used to say, and Flora said it after him, copying his sinister voice. He would have been very cross about Zeppelin's puppies because their father was either a big woolly poodle, owned by a man who manufactured motorcycle helmets, or a German shepherd which had come calling from the opposite edge of the harbor. In the past, when Anthea had visited the farm at Christmastime, old Lionel had often told her about his childhood, about dead Henry who had died when he was only ten, and about baby sister Anne, long since married and living in Australia. As he named these ghosts and told stories about the past, old Lionel would sometimes begin to cry. His voice would go on just as usual, but tears would spill out into the wrinkles around his eyes.

"It's not that I'm sad," he had once declared, sounding impatient with himself, "I just remember too much." He had badly wanted time to stand still in this cleft of childhood. Now, one of the roses, a white one, growing in a corner where roses had always been grown, had its roots in old Lionel's ashes. "Open the window and let old Lionel in," Molly used to say, meaning the scent of the roses. But Flora muttered that old Lionel still haunted the house, and blamed him because young Lionel had not yet lined the walls.

Anthea went through the hall, her hands tucked into her sleeves, comforting the mysterious scratches that had appeared overnight on the inside of her arms. She paused to look at old Lionel's portrait. Although she could remember what sort of eyes her own father had had, what sort of nose and ears and mouth, she was already finding it hard to remember just how they had all fitted together. She half hoped that she might surprise something in old Lionel's picture which would bring her father's face vividly back to her. Before she could surprise anything out of the picture, though, the door burst open behind her.

"Okay," Lionel was saying. "That's it! Countdown! Brown case, green pack, lunch, car keys. Oh, glory! Where are the car keys? I can't have lost them!" He skipped around in a mad dance, slapping at his pockets, hoping to feel the keys tucked away close to him.

"I'm always telling you to hang them up," Molly boomed

down the hall as he ran into their bedroom. Though she was not very tall, her voice was surprisingly deep. She had got as far as putting on blue jeans and Roman sandals, but still wore her striped pajama top. "Come on, everyone. Help him find his keys."

"Darling, you sound like gunfire at sea!" Lionel shouted back, booming himself. Anthea could hear him searching feverishly, shuffling things around on the bedside table, knocking them over, then swearing softly to himself.

"No keys, no car; no car, no work; no work, no money; no money, everyone *starves!*" Molly chanted, sounding both grim and mischievous.

Looking back down the hall into the big room, Anthea saw Molly run her hand down the furry spine of Glorious, and then give Flora a quick hug before she began feeling along the braces of the stripped wall in case Lionel had absentmindedly left the keys there. "What did you do when you came in last night? What was the very first thing you did?" she called.

"He might have locked them in the car," Flora suggested, standing with one shoe on and one foot held in the air to keep her clean sock clean. Lionel heard this.

"Strike down that child!" he roared back from the bedroom. "Coat her with honey and let man-eating ants crawl all over her." He had locked the keys in the car twice since Anthea had been living with them.

Suddenly, he exploded out of the bedroom waving the keys in the air. "I told you! Didn't I say?" he shouted, running back down the hall. His father's picture watched him go but, being great art, was able to watch Anthea at the same time. The door slammed. She was alone once more.

Lost at sea! Whenever Anthea was on her own even for a minute, those words floated into her head, spoken by some voice . . . not her own . . . not a voice she recognized. She couldn't even be certain if it were a man or a woman speaking. The words, coming from somewhere inside her, sounded desolate and quite sure of themselves. Yet some day, Anthea dreamed, her mother and father might be found again, shipwrecked on an island so small that no one had ever discovered it before. They would be golden-brown and slender, able to swim like fish, able to dart down through green water to pale sand at the bottom of the sea. Until they were found and buried, she couldn't help thinking they might turn up somewhere, perhaps a hundred years from now—still young and beautiful—astonished to find how much time had gone by while they were swimming. They had often been late collecting her from her baby-sitters. "The time just flew by," they would always say apologetically. She couldn't believe she wouldn't hear them say it again, someday.

Anthea's own room with the hole in the wall was no real refuge for her. She turned, instead, into the spare room, which was kept tidy for possible visitors. It was still called old Lionel's room because, although no sun reached it, it had been the family room of his childhood. Once here, the rest of the house grew faint and faraway for Anthea, and she could have a few minutes on her own.

It was a dim room looking out under the half-closed eyelid of the verandah roof. Vines that old Lionel himself had planted sprawled down over the verandah's edge, filling his room with faint and tremulous shadows. A quiver of darkness ran continually to and fro across the walls, over the old pictures, and the framed family photographs of serious-looking relations, or of children tanned by time, not summer, all grown-up now and gone away. Anthea could not name any of them. Below the photographs was a bookcase filled with boys' adventure stories, old Lionel's school prizes. Anthea had studied their faded spines many times, but she was never tempted to take them out to read.

But on this particular morning she saw something on a shadowy bottom shelf, something she had vaguely noticed several times before without ever wondering much about it. All the same it must have impressed her for it had found its way into her dream. There it was—the very box covered in the faded curtain material, green with white flowers, that the dream boy had been holding. Anthea looked at it suspiciously, wondering if the box hadn't somehow summoned her into this dim room, with its flickering walls and scents of lavender and dust. But suspicion faded. She grew curious and, sitting down on the floor, pulled the box from the bottom shelf and opened it.

Inside were a brittle notebook filled with round childish writing, a pile of cards (more photographs, she thought) held together by a red ribbon, a map drawn by hand, and a bracelet welded out of a strip of thin copper, with a pattern of holes punched into it. At the bottom lay a flat tin box made to look rather like a book, and on the front, where a book's title would have been, was printed in golden letters, *The Rotoscope Folding Stereoscopic Apparatus*. Anthea pressed a metal catch and opened the box. A triangular gold-painted frame immediately sprang up at one end. It was plainly meant to hold something, probably some sort of card. She could see the clip to hold the card in place. Lying flat in the other half of the box was something that seemed to be a mask, staring up at her with round blank glassy eyes. It was designed to be looked through . . . a viewer, thought Anthea, carefully folding it up out of its narrow bed. Once open, the box became a flat piece of dark green tin, hinged in the middle, about six inches wide and eight inches long. The card holder stood at one end, the viewer at the other.

Anthea now studied the cards tied with red ribbon, and saw they were not the family photographs she had first thought them to be. On each card, two apparently identical photographs were mounted side by side. Sliding one out from under the ribbon, she put it into the card holder and looked through the viewer, only to find she could barely make out whatever it was she was supposed to be seeing. Yet, suddenly eager, she carried it over to the window and looked again.

At first she saw two pictures (one with each eye, perhaps), but then her sight shifted in some way, and she understood that the two pictures were trying to melt together into a single picture which would have a mysterious depth to it. The flat card would suddenly blossom with hidden space. She did not have it focused quite correctly, but there was something about the blurred view that made her heart bang rather unpleasantly. Then, almost automatically, she moved the card holder by sliding it along narrow grooves on either side of the tin box. She looked again.

The photo in the frame showed the crack in the world—a jagged gash running across a snowy slope. It seemed almost lifesize, certainly much larger than the picture on the card, and incredibly clear and deep. Beside it stood the boy, facing her, pointing to the crack with one hand and in the other holding out, not the box this time, but the same stereoscope that Anthea herself held at that very moment. And it seemed to Anthea that, coming out of the crack beside him, was a hand on a scratched wrist, groping upward, just as if someone were trying to pull herself up out of the cleft. Anthea's own hand began to shake as it jerked the card holder along its tin grooves; then the picture blurred and became indistinguishable. At that moment the door creaked. Flora looked in at her.

"We're going to miss the bus if you don't hurry," she said.

"Look what I've found," said Anthea, feeling a little stupid.

Flora looked, but was not surprised. She had seen it before.

"Henry's stereoscope," she said. "Old Lionel inherited it. 3D television of ancient times."

"Henry?" asked Anthea. Flora had spoken as if everyone knew who Henry was, but Anthea had to be reminded.

"Lionel's brother! Dead Henry. That one there!" Flora pointed at one of the old photographs over the bookcase. Sure enough, there he stood, holding the stereoscope, just as she had seen him a moment ago on the edge of the crack in the world. He smiled a little—triumphantly—she thought, like someone who has a space all his own, held safely between his own two hands. But it seemed to her this was a space he was offering to share.

Chapter 3

AFTER SCHOOL, Anthea and Flora had to catch the school bus and travel most of the way home with a lot of other children. Flora always rather enjoyed the bus ride. She shouted abuse at the boys, flicked pellets of paper at enemies, and boldly pulled faces at the bus driver's back when he told them to quiet down. But then the bus would stop. Anthea and Flora would get off, just the two of them, and walk along a narrow country road, up over a little hill, and down the long drive between the walnut trees. The old house waited for them, slumped among its orchards, gardens, and tumbledown sheds. In front of them, as they came over the hill, lay the harbor with the dragon-shaped island. The peninsula, Wakefield's Point, known among the family as Old Daisy because it looked so much like a lopsided, long-haired woman diving—sketched eastward toward the mouth of the harbor.

As Flora walked, she swung her school pack from side to side and complained about school, getting back into her own skin before she arrived home again. The late afternoon sun beat down strongly on her hands and face.

"Mrs. Phelps," said Flora. "Mrs. Phelps!" She screwed up her face and spoke in a mincing voice that was supposed to be like the voice of Mrs. Phelps, her teacher. "Flora, let's try to have a little hush at the back there. Flora, don't click that ballpoint pen while I'm talking."

She began to whistle, and then stopped to look sideways at Anthea.

"How come *you* never get told off?" she asked, sounding a little resentful.

"I don't know," Anthea said.

"I *want* to argue," declared Flora proudly, "I'm practising for politics."

Flora was planning to be New Zealand's first woman prime minister when she grew up.

"You get all those trips abroad," she said, "and you don't have to eat health food."

"Or have dreams," Anthea said. Compared with her dream of the crack in the world, the hills, the sea, and the old house looked as bright and flat as pictures on a travel poster.

"Everyone has dreams," Flora said, "and if someone wakes you up in the middle of your dreams you die." She loved inventing alarming theories like that in a second. "You might be going to walk in your sleep again," she added enviously.

Since she had come to live in the old house, Anthea had woken several times to find herself not in the bed in which she had gone to sleep—with Flora just through the hole in the wall—but in some other place. Once she was standing among hills of earth planted with courgettes in Molly's vegetable garden; another time she was trying to climb the linen-cupboard shelves and had pulled a great pile of sheets, pillow cases, and tea towels down on herself. Flora was jealous of Anthea's sleepwalking.

"You're too romantic," she had cried, "what with having long hair *and* being an orphan *and* sleepwalking."

Remembering this, Flora swung her pack so fiercely that it suddenly unfastened itself on one side and spread pencils and sheets of paper across the road.

They stared at each other. Then Flora's mouth twisted into a silly smile and she laughed. That made it all right for Anthea to laugh, too. It was an odd thing about Flora . . . just when you thought you knew what she was going to do, she did something else.

"You looked so scared I had to laugh," Flora said.

"I thought you might explode," Anthea answered.

"I thought I was going to," Flora said proudly.

It was the second time that day that they had laughed together at the same thing.

When they were home they looked for Zeppelin and found her drowsing on the verandah. She had not had her puppies yet.

Flora stood staring down at her and sighed with discontent. "Sometimes I think we're stuck in time, everything on the way but never getting here," she complained. "By the time these puppies come out they'll be dogs wearing collars."

"Let's bring that stereoscope out on to the verandah," Anthea suggested in a sly, dreamy voice.

"That old thing!" said Flora scornfully. "I suppose it seemed great in the days when they didn't have TV."

"But I haven't seen it properly," explained Anthea.

"Oh, well. Okay . . . and we can have something to eat," added Flora.

"I'm just getting a couple of biscuits, Molly," she called to her mother, who was weeding around the lemon trees under the kitchen window. But secretly she took three biscuits each. Then she filled two glasses with fruit juice, balanced the biscuits on top of them, and came out to find Anthea had already brought out the fabric-covered box and was sorting through its contents. She had slid the bracelet with the punched holes in it up on to her own arm, and was studying the notebook.

"There's an arrow drawn on it," she said. "Look! An arrow with a funny head."

"It's an eye!" Flora pointed out. "It's an arrow that can see where it's meant to go."

Anthea spread the cards out as if she were telling fortunes with them. The stereoscope lay quietly at her elbow.

Flora plumped down on the wobbly chair; and they sat eating biscuits, occasionally dunking them in their fruit juice, while they took turns in looking at the pictures. Flora found herself fascinated, almost against her will, by the moment when the two flat pictures fused into one deep one. The scenes filled out with a space that did not really exist—space that could be folded up into a box that looked like a book; space that could become as flat as a bookmark and as easily hidden away. For all that, the scenes were lifeless. Life in these pictures was replaced with a sort of *waiting*.

"Very suspicious!" declared Flora, studying a picture of soldiers looking out of trenches or through coils of barbed wire and bleak mounds of upturned earth. "They look as if they've stopped in the middle of doing something because they know we're looking at them."

"What's this one?" Anthea asked a moment later. "Is it a castle somewhere?"

She was looking into a great room with a geometrical mosaic running around its walls, and doorways shaped like huge keyholes.

"Put it in the ancient monument pile," commanded Flora, who had automatically begun to put the cards in some sort of order. She patted a pile of cards with the picture of a Roman coliseum on top of it, looking critically at another card as she did so. "This one isn't anything much. I wonder why they put it in." Anthea took it from her, and slid it into the stereoscope.

Compared with some of the other cards, it was certainly unremarkable: a lake or perhaps a harbor very similar to their own. Tall cliffs strained back from the water, and in the distance, the line of an island straggled and hunched like a dragon hiding itself in the sea. There was a dangerous look to the water, eating itself into a lacy pattern at the foot of the cliff. Through the stereoscope you could see spray hanging above the rocks—spray which never fell into the water that streamed in perfect stillness back toward the sea. Whether the spray had been skimmed by some strong wind or had exploded upward after a breaking wave, no one could tell. Further out, the pictured water was as glassy as their own harbor often looked, early in the morning before the wind got up. This picture was bland, but sinister, as well. Sea gulls hung in the air, unnaturally still above the sculptured lace of the foam. Though the island gave the impression of being ancient and difficult to reach, it also looked as if it might be restful once you did reach it. Anthea, whose pulse had quickened at the sight of its empty beaches, imagined pulling a small dinghy up onto the sand; imagined searching for shells, staring at the sea, and lighting a campfire before setting out into the unexplored interior, and all in wonderful silence and solitude. She dreamed, and as she dreamed, felt the afternoon sun scorching her cheek and her arm, even though it was so late in the day.

"What about *this* one!" Flora was exclaiming. "Isn't this one spooky?"

And indeed it was a strange picture. On a black octagonal plinth stood the bust of a woman, her face bent forward a little and draped entirely in a veil caught in and knotted under her chin. Through the veil Anthea could see that the woman's eyes were closed, could make out the line of her nose and the curve of her lips.

"Who is it?" she asked, turning the card over. *Statuary*, said the print on the back. *New Zealand Exhibition; Modesty* and then E. BEARDSLEY: *Importer of Photographic Requisites*.

"Modesty!" Flora cried, reading over her shoulder. "I'd hate to be that modest."

Anthea thought there was no danger of Flora ever veiling her face and bowing her head in silence. Besides, though E. Beardsley might have been a real photographer, and the statue in the picture might have really been called *Modesty*, she immediately believed that, in stereoscope space, *Sadness* would be its true name. If you lifted the veil you would see the stone eyes were swollen and red and the stone nose was running. "You go ahead and cry, dear," someone had said to her when they knew her parents must be dead. But they only wanted her to cry for a little while and then stop. Crying got on people's nerves. Nobody wanted to look at a sad, swollen face for long. That was why this woman had put on a veil.

"Shove it in with ancient monuments," Flora ordered. "It isn't a museum and it isn't war, or Spain or anything. Then try this one. This is my favorite."

Storm clouds rolled behind low hills in the distance. In the foreground, wild horses galloped, shoulder to shoulder, across an eerie plain, one black horse just a little ahead of the rest.

"Terrific," Anthea said. "Think of riding a wild horse!"

Flora had often thought of it. From the time she had first been allowed to use the stereoscope, this picture had seemed to hold all the beauty and wildness of the world. She had often imagined herself to be part of that wildness, riding on that leading black horse, its mane blowing out behind it, while her own hair blew back in a dark cloud. Only when she had stopped looking through the mask, did Flora remember, with confusion and surprise, that she had short mouse-colored hair which, even in a storm would only bob around her ears. Anthea's hair, though, would certainly stream around her, pale against the storm clouds, as she went galloping . . . galloping . . .

"I suppose we'd only fall off," Flora said, sounding very practical, "and the other horses would tread all over us." And she put the picture of the wild horses in a pile that she had privately labeled Nature. "What's the next one?"

"We've come back to the beginning," Anthea said. Flora peered into the stereoscope at the last card which had also been the first. But, though there was something about the picture which teased her memory, she did not recognize the crack in the world from Anthea's dream. Besides, there was no boy standing next to it today.

"You know, if you got on to the right road," she said, "it would take you to all these places. Most of them have got a road in them. You could visit them all."

"There's no road in the Modesty one," Anthea argued.

Flora continued to peer at the crack in the world, for it certainly reminded her of something, though she couldn't

think what. "That's because it's at the *beginning* of the journey," she said, inventing. "The road comes *after*."

Then they heard the sound of a car roaring toward them.
Lionel was driving homeward between the walnut trees.

"Gosh, listen!" Flora said. "He's in the wrong gear. He's
a rotten driver." She could not drive herself but felt sure she
had already worked out the rules. Dropping the cards, she
took off across the verandah, down the steps, and over the
grass, so that by the time Lionel had parked his car and struggled out of it, Flora was beside him shouting, "You were
accelerating in second gear!" and leaping up at him, ready to
be hugged.

Anthea looked away from them, pausing before collaps-
ing the stereoscope into its green tin, and packing the box
again. She slid the bracelet off, noticing that her arm was
slightly sunburnt and that the bracelet had left its pattern burnt
on to her skin. She dropped it into the box. Then she picked
up the notebook, imagining it to be full of secret arrows that
withered away and fell in a fine powder from between its
pages. She opened it. The writing was rusty black and
scratchy, formed years ago with an old-fashioned dip-pen.

The secret land of Viridian, she read, *is the opposite of all other
lands because everywhere else has the sea around it, but Viridian has
the sea in the middle. This sea has salt and tides and waves that go
out in all directions from the center, and the heart of the sea is an
island. If you run away to sea in Viridian you run into the middle,
not out to the edge. Say the mystic passwords "Nai di Riv" and you
will begin your journey.*

"Nai di riv?" Anthea said aloud. They were clumsy words to say, but as she said them she understood that they were Viridian spelled backward.

Anthea thought this might be a message that was intended for her alone. She read the paragraph over again, only vaguely hearing Lionel in the background. Then she slipped the notebook into her pocket. I'll look at it later, she thought, but in reality she knew she was stealing it.

"Face it, Flora, you wouldn't recognize second gear if it came up and kissed you good morning," Lionel was saying, climbing the steps with his little green pack in one hand and his office case in the other. He and Flora jostled and laughed in the doorway. Anthea waited until they were well through, and then followed them.

That night, turning her back on the hole in the wall, with Flora yawning on the other side of it, she remembered the notebook and the message in its careful childish printing. She put her hand under the pillow and touched the notebook hidden there.

"What rubbish!" she thought to herself, and soon afterward fell sound asleep.

Chapter 4

AT SOME TIME during the night Anthea found she was staring at a hand . . . staring right *into* it, past the skin, past the wonderful embroidery of its blood vessels and nerves, to the very bones themselves, spread out against a pattern of red and white. All of this seemed to be nothing to do with the hand itself.

"When did I wake up?" she thought, not frightened but astonished, still staring into the hand which reminded her of something. A house somewhere. Yes! Stripped of their smooth outer surfaces, hands, like houses, were all pipes and electrical wiring and joists. But then the transparent hand clouded from within, and rapidly became a real hand with fingernails and familiar stains of a purple felt pen on the second finger. She recognized a mark left over from last night's homework. It was her own hand she was staring at, and it lay against an extraordinary wall.

Because she was so close to it, Anthea could see the lines where square slabs of marble had been fitted together, but from a little distance this wall would look as if it were carved out of a single piece of stone. From the floor up to the level of her eyes, it was heavily inlaid in red and silver. Circles and stars spun toward her, passed under her hand, and spun away, circle after circle, star after star. As her puzzled eyes ran along this endless inlaid pattern, it began to wheel around, hesitantly at first, then faster and faster, and something inside her began to wheel with it. So, Anthea and the pattern, neither of them moving an inch, somehow spun together until the pattern ran into a high narrow doorway with an arched top, a doorway more like an immense keyhole than a door. The pattern spun away on the other side of this doorway, but Anthea, set free from it now, looked up and around. She was standing in a second doorway—a wider one. Double arches above her head were supported in the middle by a marble column. Straight ahead lay a vast empty hall and, in the distance, double doors of heavy black wood. She was the only living thing there. Anthea suddenly had more space to herself than she had ever had in her life before. There was a faint tap on the floor beside her, but she was occupied with taking in all this space, so new and yet somehow familiar, and did not notice it.

The high-arched ceiling was inlaid with a tiny, dense repetitive pattern. Under her feet, which were wearing their sensible school sandals, lay slabs of foggy gray marble. Across the squares her shadow lay, stretched in front of her, pale but distinct. And there, beside it, lay another shadow, thrown by someone taller than she, someone standing just behind her.

She could make out a head and sloping shoulders, but no arms or legs. The faint tap came again, and this time Anthea not only heard it but saw what had caused it. A drop of water had splashed on the gray marble, vanishing at once because it was too transparent to be seen against the grayness.

Slowly turning, prickling with fear as she turned, Anthea remembered the old Arabian story of a prince who had had half his body turned into marble by his wicked wife. However, the shape casting the shadow was stone all the way through. A head and shoulders, larger than lifesize, were set on a tall black plinth. The head, a woman's head, was wrapped in a veil that covered not only her face but her hair. Though the veil was made of stone, it was so fine that Anthea could make out the features of the face behind it.

As she stared at it apprehensively, moisture soaked through the veil. A drop of water slowly gathered on one of the folds as if the stone face behind the stone veil were crying.

The weeping stone, the pattern of stars and circles, and the keyhole-shaped doorways all seemed familiar, but Anthea's memories were watery ghosts of what they should have been. Her parents, Molly, Flora, and Lionel swam through her thoughts, and she recognized them in a clouded way, as characters in a story she had read when she was very young, but which were faded now by time and tears. Flora was stronger and brighter than anyone else, but even she was more like a shape moving on the other side of a clouded glass than a real girl. The gathering tear fell, and another one began to form at once. Anthea shivered and turned her back on the weeping stone. She did not really want to guess at the face behind the veil. Instead, she walked out into the space in front of her, and the hushed echo of her own footsteps scuttled around the walls ahead of her and on either side. It was as if several other Antheas were advancing down the empty hall toward the black doors.

When she was out into the space of the hall Anthea saw that there were windows in the walls on either side of her, each window set deep in the thickness of the wall and framed by tall slender pillars. After a little hesitation she drifted over to the nearest window, leaned on the deep sill and looked out. There was nothing to see but sky, so she hitched herself further across the deep sill and looked down.

There was land somewhere far below her, but it seemed to be blotted out by heavy shifting mist, occasionally pierced by gleaming peaks, white blades sharpened by wind and light. Anthea screwed up her face, frowning, just as she did over mathematical puzzles at school. She was looking down on mountain tops, and to look down on them she realized she must be above them, perhaps on the highest mountain of all. She moved on to the next window and then on to another, and at last found she could see something apart from sky and mist and the slicing peaks. There were two ragged breaks in the mist, peepholes like those on the viewer of a stereoscope, and through them she saw the gleam of water and the dragonish shape of an island, dark but outlined in light as if an early morning sun had run a pen around its edges. Anthea knew at once that this was a place she wanted to get to, a place she knew about already. For instance, she knew—she *seemed* to know—that it was wound around with a golden beach where people could sunbathe, that there were rocks to dive from and that the water, as unresisting as green air, would be crossed by fish as beautiful as birds. She also knew it was a long way off and wondered vaguely about the veiled country that must lie between her and her island. It must slope downhill all the way, she thought, slope gently but surely, right to the water's edge.

At last, with a sigh, she turned away from the window, and drifted into the center of the hall again. A black smudge in the middle of the immaculate gray floor caught her eye. She moved toward it.

An arrow with a sharp oval for a head pointed toward the door. Someone had drawn a black slit from side to side of the oval, turning it into an eye, so that the arrow not only directed her on, but looked at her as it did so. Anthea frowned, then touched it curiously, feeling it warmer than the stone, and slightly greasy under her fingers. It seemed to have been drawn with a thick, black crayon.

There are some dreams when you suddenly know you are dreaming, and feel you can choose between waking up and going on with the dream. Looking dubiously at the eye which was also an arrow, Anthea felt tempted to let herself wake up. But then a whisper crept across the floor toward her. She looked up and saw that the huge black doors were moving, swinging inward. A narrow shaft of light struck across the floor toward her. Sinking back into her dream once more, Anthea marched over to the door and seized its handle in both hands, tugging it so that it sighed again and swung wide, letting in a flood of sunshine.

Dazzling light enveloped her. A sudden gust of wind, so cold it was like being slashed with a blade of ice, cut across her face and took her breath away for a moment. There was no sign of the heavy mist she had seen through the window. Instead, she was looking into space without limits, distance without edges, no horizon at all, until she looked down, and saw how the world fell away at her very feet. There was a narrow, almost vertical stairway, more like a ladder cut into the stone than stairs. Then the mountains began, fold after fold of silent white slopes, falling down to shingle beds which tumbled in turn to wooded hills so far away it seemed it would take her weeks to reach them. Still sloping, the countryside stretched itself out into a long curve and, at last, at the very edge of sight, she saw the lake. She could not quite make out where land ended and water began, for there seemed to be some sort of a cloud, a dirty grayish billowing cloud on the hazy boundary. Beyond the cloud the dragonish island glittered like a tiny jewel and waited for her.

"It's not a lake. It's the sea," Anthea whispered, unwilling to break the white silence around her, though suddenly she could hear the wind blowing over the snow and wondered why, apart from that first gust, she could not feel it.

Just where the stairway ended, a wide well cared for road began. There, where everything else was wild and untouched, was a road, unsurfaced but graded and smooth, looping around the first sharp slopes of the mountain peak, inviting her to follow it.

Earlier, Anthea knew she had longed for limitless space. Now, the immensity of the sky alone seemed too much. She quite wanted to get down among the folds of the mountains, to feel just a little contained by the world rather than marooned above it. Yet, though she was lured by the road, quite unexpectedly she found she did not want to be the only traveler. Then she saw, drawn in black crayon on a white stone, another arrow with an eye by way of a head. So she stepped over the threshold and began a journey.

As she did so, the doors sighed and swung firmly shut behind her. Anthea turned and pushed against them, just to make sure of what she already knew . . . that, now she was on the road, there was no going back. The doors did not budge, any more than the mountain would have budged and, as the sunlight fell on her, Anthea felt it beginning to dissolve her out of one place and into another. This time there was no choice. Her eyes, which had seemed to be wide open, were actually closed, and when she opened them she was looking up into the skeleton roof above her bed, with Flora peering intently at her through the hole in the wall.

"What were you saying?" Flora asked curiously.

"I don't know," Anthea said, pretending to be sleepier than she was. She buried her face in her pillow, already longing for it to be nighttime once more, for at that moment the journey of the dream seemed more real than the pipes, wiring, and struts of everyday life.

Chapter 5

"WHERE'S MOLLY?" Flora asked, coming through the bead curtain and finding Lionel in the kitchen, carefully cutting his own sandwiches. His lunches were important to him, and he always wrapped his sandwiches tenderly, before tucking them into their plastic box.

"I sent her outside with Teddy, just to look at the morning for a while," Lionel said. "What's the use of living in the most beautiful place in the world if you're always too busy to look at it? Where's Anthea?"

"I don't know. Mooning around somewhere!" said Flora. "She can get her own lunch."

Flora and her father dived backward and forward past one another, searching for the things they liked best. Lionel had had a good start, but Flora finished first. She did not take lunch as seriously as he did.

"What are you having?" he asked, looking anxiously at her box, just in case her lunch was better than his.

"A little box of raisins, an orange and apple, a piece of

cheese, and two biscuits," Flora said. "Well, three biscuits, actually!"

"Why don't you have jam sandwiches?" asked Lionel. "We made all that jam, and no one ever uses it."

"I don't like jam," Flora answered. "I told you I didn't like jam, but you said we had to use the plums."

"We have twenty pots of jam turning into a sort of plum-flavored rubber in the back of the pantry," Lionel cried. "We're supposed to be self-sufficient, and that means using up our own jam."

"Have *you* got jam sandwiches?" Flora asked, accusingly.

"Of course," he replied, but he put his hand guiltily on the lid of his lunch box as he spoke.

"Where's the jam pot, then?" Flora demanded, looking around suspiciously. Lionel grinned to himself. "You have *not* got jam sandwiches," she cried accusingly.

"Have so!" he said, still grinning as he quickly pushed his lunch box into his little green pack, which was on the floor next to his lean businessman's case. Lionel always carried his pens, calculator, papers, and graphs in the brown case, while his lunch and detective story went in the green pack, along with a clean tie and shoe-cleaning stuff. For every morning he did a strange thing. He drove up to the top of the hill and finished dressing there.

"There's no sense in polishing my shoes at home," he said. "By the time I've got out of the car to open the gate, got back into it to drive it through, and *out* of it again to *shut* the gate, my shoes are covered with mud—sometimes worse if any cows have gone by. Now, would *you* trust an accountant up to his ankles in cow dung?"

Flora was always fascinated to see her father change from being easygoing Lionel into something both sleeker and sharper. He would brush the biddibids from the cuffs of his trousers, take off his sloppy jersey, and slide himself into the suit jacket that always hung in the back of his car on a red plastic coat hanger. Then he would polish his shoes very carefully and put on his tie, and as he polished and tied, he seemed to polish and tie himself in other ways, too. His expression sharpened. His movements grew neater and more controlled. Lionel had an east-of-the-hills life, and a west-of-the-hills life, and knotting the tie up on the hill above his home was the sign of a change in his head as he went from being one thing to another.

"Talking of self-sufficiency," he went on, "how about giving Molly a break? Mix the hens' mash for her!"

Flora could not see the verandah but, if she listened, she could hear a sharp irregular tapping somewhere outside the kitchen. The hens were pecking at the glass, longing for someone to come out and feed them.

"I've already fed the cats, Anthea's cat, too!" Flora cried. "Why do *I* have to feed the hens?"

"It's dirty, dangerous work, but someone has to do it," Lionel said in the voice of a television soldier.

"Well, Anthea could take a turn," Flora argued. "She

doesn't do anything, *ever*." However, she was already getting the plastic mash bowl from under the sink. "It's not *fair*," she grumbled.

Lionel had been about to leave the kitchen, but now he stopped and turned and said mildly, "I know it's not fair. I wish it were. But we—Molly and I, that is—want to give her just a little bit longer to settle down before we start nagging at her like we nag at you."

"It isn't fair," Flora repeated stubbornly.

"Nothing's fair," Lionel pointed out, leaning in the doorway as if he needed something to prop him up. The bead curtain trembled in a sort of brown storm behind him. "It's not fair to Anthea that she has to come and pig it out in the country with us. It's not fair that we've got each other, and she hasn't got anyone."

"She's got us," Flora snapped. "Don't we count?"

"Not yet," Lionel replied, sighing. "Maybe never!"

"Yes, but . . . " began Flora. "I know all that but . . . she *lives* here and her *cat* lives here and she forgets to feed it and wash its bowl. And it's chased my cat away. Poor Taffeta, out in the cold. No fire to sit by."

"Flora . . . it's midsummer," Lionel pointed out. "Taffeta spends a lot of her summers out in the garden anyway."

"She thinks she's better than us," Flora grumbled. "Anthea, I mean, not Taffeta. I see her giving stuck-up looks at our pig bucket."

"I wouldn't worry unless the bucket starts to give snooty looks back," Lionel said, glancing toward the door anxiously in case Anthea might be on the other side of the bead curtain, listening.

"She's not there. She won't even be on the sundeck," Flora said, looking a little guilty. (She often tried to make the old house seem smarter by calling the verandah the sundeck.) "She's frightened of the rooster."

"Well, go and talk to her. Bring eggs into the conversation casually," Lionel suggested. "And then mention that you're going to mix the mash. Maybe she'll offer to help you this time around."

"Not likely!" muttered Flora. All the same, she left the kitchen, and searched for Anthea who turned out to be in the spare room, standing by the window and peering into the old stereoscope for the second morning running.

"I'm going to mix the *hens' mash*," said Flora loudly.

Anthea did not offer to help, but just stood, dreamily folding the stereoscope back into its tin box once more. But she asked an unexpected question.

"Who used to play with this?"

"*They* did, I suppose," said Flora. "Dead Henry and old Lionel and Great Aunt Anne."

"I've almost forgotten what he was like," Anthea said. "Grandad, I mean!"

Flora frowned and tried to remember old Lionel.

"He didn't want us to change anything about the house," she said. "He was really crabby when we put in the woodstove. He said the fireplace was enough. He said that if the house had needed a woodstove he'd have put one in himself.

Oh, well," she went on, with an elaborate sigh, "I'd better go and *feed the hens*."

"Okay. See you in a minute," said Anthea, leafing through the stereoscope cards as if her thoughts were already miles away. She'd lived there for six months, but still did not seem to realize how much it helped to have someone stirring the mash while water was poured into it.

"It's too gloomy in here to see the cards properly," Flora said. "We're going to put in new big windows all along this wall when Lionel finds the time." The faint leafy shadows quivered as if they were alive and listening.

"I'm just checking up on something," Anthea muttered vaguely. So Flora marched out, stepping down the hall and under her grandfather's picture, glancing sharply up at him as she passed. She always did. On this particular morning she saw something she had sometimes seen before and always feared to see. The painted green eyes of the portrait were turned away from her, looking toward the front door.

Flora felt a peculiar sense of being stifled which meant that she was beginning to be frightened. She knew what the portrait was looking at and had tried to tell her parents, but no one ever took her seriously. Indeed, struggling to put it into words somehow stopped her from believing it herself. Lionel and Molly merely joked about the house being haunted, but Flora knew it was true.

"Oh, all right!" she hissed impatiently, because she hated being frightened, particularly when the ghost had never harmed her. She turned around crossly and stared toward the front door. There it was, watching her, a shadowy figure, a boy of her own age or perhaps a little older, a patch of darkness, but transparent, the colors of the stained glass showing through him. He didn't do anything . . . just watched her in silence.

"All right!" Flora hissed again. "Nobody's going to put in new windows. Have it your way!" At the sound of her hiss, the figure began to dissolve as if he had been nothing but an odd trick of the morning light. Within a minute there was nothing left of him.

Flora looked sternly up at her grandfather's portrait. Now, it had become true art once more and returned her gaze unwaveringly. Shrugging, she set off, walking in a firm unfrightened self-sufficient way, to mix the mash on her own.

Chapter 6

OVER THE NEXT TWO NIGHTS Anthea dreamed again, walking deeper and deeper into her dreams. Once there, time changed. She seemed to remember wandering for day after day in an unhurried tranquil fashion, and wondered if, while she was busy at school or sitting in the bus with Flora, some part of her was still journeying down from the mountains.

At first, the road was so steep that she moved with small, careful steps. She was surrounded by a whiteness that made big distances seem small, and small distances immense. Such purity made it impossible to judge time or space. Besides, the mountains, the road, Anthea herself, were all engulfed in a silence that was also timeless. It was true that the wind occasionally whined like a dog at her heels, but that one sound only made the quietness of snow and sky grow in power. All around her the land which she thought might be called Viridian, fell in serene white folds. The aching blue of the sky and the blackness of her own footsteps left in the crust of snow, were the only colors to be seen on the road, a road

44

which felt more and more like home. Of course home was
usually a place where people stayed put, whereas the road
kept Anthea moving on.

For two nights Anthea dreamed of this timeless road and
wanted nothing more. However, going to bed on Thursday
night and sliding her hand under the pillow to check on the
hidden notebook, she found herself half-hoping that something different might happen in tonight's dreaming. She was
a little shocked at herself. It almost seemed disloyal. Then she
closed her eyes, and immediately heard, faint but clear, a
sound she remembered with dismay: tap, tap, tap . . . water
dripping slowly and steadily—never once stopping.

Anthea imagined at once that the statue from the hall on
the top of the mountains might be following her, weeping as
it came, for the tapping sounded like tears falling onto crisp
snow. It was not falling tears, however. Somewhere, an icicle
had begun to melt, and as her dream took shape around her
she found the roadside echoing with watery sounds. Not just
one icicle, but all of them, dripped busily. Tiny energetic rills
began to carve their way down through the whiteness. Slowly,
as she followed the road, the pure unchanging crystalline
world that had first comforted her began dissolving into a
busy gushing flowing countryside, alive with torrents and
waterfalls, while tussocks of coarse tawny grass, breaking free
from the quilt of snow, tossed in winds which Anthea could
hear but not feel. Now, the road flattened a little so that her
feet were no longer pointing quite so sharply downward, nor
feeling quite so constantly for contact with treacherous angles.

And then the road began to rise and fall as if the land were breathing peacefully beneath it. Anthea was still able to see a vast panorama from a series of hilltops; to gaze along valleys and across moorland to distant peaks that just might belong to lost cities filled with silver towers, but more probably were spurs belonging to other mountain ranges. Below and beyond, she could still make out the gleam of that faraway water and the glittering island no bigger than an emblem on the head of a pin. There was no hurry to get there. It would not go away. She was free to stand and stare for as long as she liked in this musically rushing countryside, knowing that no voice would call her for school or dinner, or suggest, with heavy meaning, that she might mix the hens' mash. Whole minutes, or maybe hours, went by, while she dreamily welcomed a space that was all her own.

After a while, she even had company of a sort, for all the streams ran together into a swift, fierce little river. The road followed the river and Anthea followed the road, though sometimes a meadow full of hardy wildflowers, or a clump of trees, made her pause and wonder if perhaps she shouldn't set out across country. She traveled on (she thought) for days, neither sleeping nor wanting to sleep, but more and more she caught herself listening for a voice—any voice—and half-longing for a sight of some fellow traveler. There were never any traces of footsteps or wheels in the snow, or in the mud on the side of the road but, after all, it *was* a road, and a road usually meant a country council somewhere. She might come across a road mender with a bulldozer, spreading gravel over

icy corners. Roads did not look after themselves. Yet, deep
down, Anthea could not quite believe in the road mender.
She had the odd feeling that, even if she did reach a city or
a village, she would find it deserted.

Of course, she knew that there was at least one other
person on the road. Every now and then she would pass an
arrow, drawn into patches of snow, or crayoned on to stones
by the roadside—an arrow with an eye for a head, each one
watching her go by. Wanting some sort of company, knowing
that there was someone on the road ahead, kept her from
wandering off to the right or left. Someone was pointing the
way.

During the days that separated dream from dream, Anthea went to school, speaking when she was spoken to, eating
and drinking, and wondering when Zeppelin would have her
puppies. She never gave anyone a clue that somehow she had
found her way into a space so small it could be carried in a
tin box, yet so big it could hold halls with doorways like
keyholes and even a whole range of mountains; would hold
a wind that could be heard but not felt, together with a road,
and the promise of an ocean with an island in the middle of
it. Sometimes (when she was sure she would not be interrupted), she would take the notebook from its hiding place
under her mattress, and try to decipher the black words written by the long-ago pen. They seemed to be mostly notes for
a story in which two heroes, Sir Leo and Sir Griff battled
dragons in mountain passes, or up and down the steps of
echoing coliseums. The words were faint and hard to under-

stand. *The hero is careful,* she read. *He does not want to be swallowed by any dragon. He looks before he leaps.* The edges of the notebook flaked away between her fingers like delicate pastry.

Once she was on the road, with that other crowded life grown faint and unreal, Anthea felt completely alive, and certain she was going in the right direction. "Deeper in!" she said aloud with satisfaction.

Then, coming down through the flowing, dripping countryside around a long slow bend in the road, she suddenly found the river vanishing into a rocky gorge. The road, dotted with round smooth boulders, as if it had been flooded at some time in the past, followed the river obediently.

It was not fear of a flood, though, that made Anthea hesitate. It was the steepness of the high walls and the feeling that once you were in the gorge you might be ambushed or trapped between them. She imagined herself running wildly between those walls pursued by something . . . a giant rooster perhaps. She laughed aloud and, as she laughed, noticed a flat pale stone at head height on the canyon wall, and the arrow in black crayon drawn right across it. The eye, forming the head of the arrow, seemed to welcome her, so she walked in and out among the boulders and on into the canyon.

The walls sloped upward to shoulder height, then climbed steeply until they were far above her head. Buckled layers of rock undulated beside her like serpents, some more worn than others. At times, harder rocks would curve out over her head like shelves, and these outcrops worried her, because anything could be lying on top of them watching her approach, winding

itself up, ready to spring on her. Yet the only living things
she had seen in Viridian so far had been lichens, grasses,
tussocks, and distant trees. Nothing with teeth or a beak.
Nothing that could spring. A line of sky ran above her, looking
as if someone had squeezed it out of a tube. Frantically waving
fingers of grass scrabbled at the blue edge. It wasn't clear to
Anthea just why she was so frightened. She grumbled at herself, almost as Flora might have grumbled had she been there.

"What's wrong? There's nothing to be frightened of.
Nothing! Don't be such a wimp!"

Then it seemed that perhaps she herself was the frightening thing, that the rocks and grasses were watching her in
horror, straining back from her in case she touched them. This
was the most alarming thought of all.

"Stop it!" she cried aloud to the air.

"Stop! Stop! Stop!" the old rocks shouted back at her. She
did stop, stopped as sharply as if she were pressed against a
glass wall—terrified of the rocks and the worm of sky writhing
above her and of what she might be turning into.

The fan of reddish rock under which she stood was scalloped at the edge by wind and weather. There were golden
streaks in it, half-transparent, though not clear as glass was
clear. Looking up at it, Anthea heard a tiny sound . . . a *rolling*
sound, and something fell over the scalloped rim, tumbling
through the air so inconspicuously she almost missed it as it
fell past her and in among the stones.

"Someone's dropping spiders on me," Anthea thought,
and believed it, although she knew, with the sensible part of

her mind, that spiders did not make a rolling sound and that even big spiders were mostly harmless. Nevertheless, something about swollen spiderish bodies hanging between eight scuttling legs had always made her flinch. Flora, though, had never been frightened of spiders. She would let a spider run across her hands shouting, "Look! Look! Isn't it terrific!" She *saved* spiders when they got into the house, carrying them outside to let them go, praising them for their webs and for the silken nurseries they wove on gorsebushes for their babies. But Anthea was not Flora and, no matter how childish it might be, she remained frightened of spiders. She stood there, deliberately not looking for almost a minute. Then, gathering up her courage, she pretended to glance casually toward the river, stealing first a furtive glance at whatever it was that had dropped among the stones beside her. Her heart jolted as it would never have done for a spider. Lying at her feet was a fat black crayon.

Chapter 7

IT WAS AS IF FLORA'S HEART JOLTED. Starting awake she found, to her amazement, that she was already sitting up in bed, mouth open with alarm. On the other side of the hole in the wall, Anthea made a small gasping sound, but she was certainly sound asleep. So what was it that had frightened Flora into waking up? Everything around her seemed to be in place. Faint moonlight from a young moon reflected in through her window, touching her books and her wild horse poster. Her birthday cards were still pinned up, though her birthday had come and gone months ago. On the window ledge stood her jar of felt pens and markers, and beside them her bottle of gold ink for doing particularly grand headings for school projects (*Life in the Dessert* she had once written incorrectly in curling golden letters, with a drawing of a golden camel underneath the words). Everything was as it should be.

"What a dream!" she told herself briskly, though she could not remember dreaming anything. The fright didn't fit her at all. It felt as if it should belong to someone else.

But now she was properly awake, Flora felt hungry. Last night's dinner, tomorrow morning's breakfast, seemed equally distant. She was stuck in between them, starving. The moment she thought of breakfast she began to long for toast, but stolen midnight toast would mean brushing her teeth for the second time in the same evening, and that would mean turning on a tap, and *that* meant the pipes would clank and shudder so that Molly would probably wake up and come to investigate. In the end Flora decided an apple would have to do. She scrambled out of bed and padded out into the hall, closing her door behind her.

The hall was completely dark. The drooping eyelid of the verandah roof outside held the moonlight at bay, and the richly colored glass in the door sealed the hall still further. However, Flora knew the way by heart. She put out her hand, groping toward the door of the big room, then stopped. The familiar hall smell—a mixture of lavender floor polish, carpet shampoo, a little mildew, and all kinds of kitchen cooking smells that crept in under the door from the big room—was gone. She could smell earth. She could smell wetness. The air whispered and babbled with a sound she recognized but could not name at once. Then the picture of the garden tap came into her mind. What she was hearing in the dark was trickling water, and the whisper that ran along under it was the sound of a flowing river. Flora put out her hand in the darkness and immediately touched something hard and cold and clammy.

In fact what she felt was ordinary enough. But it was quite impossible for it to be there, in the hall, under old Lionel's picture. No matter how Flora tried to convince her hand that it had made a mistake, her hand insisted that it was touching an uneven stone wall. Under her bare feet she could feel cold striking up through sharp grit and pebbles. Wildly, she flung out her arms on either side. The knuckles of her right hand struck rocks, while the left waved in a wild, wet, murmuring space. Flora shuffled sideways. Her fingertips grazed another rough surface on the left. She was standing between rocky walls, and the aching knuckles of her right hand proved it.

"You're safe," someone breathed. "You're still in my house." Flora saw a line of light, as straight as if drawn with a ruler. It climbed until it was taller than a man, then turned and ran at right angles to itself. She drew her fingers back from the rocks, reached toward the line of light, and found herself touching a familiar surface. She pushed. There was a click and a door swung open. She was looking into the big room and could see, almost as if it were a scene on the stereoscope, her father Lionel slumped behind the big table, sound asleep with his glasses lying crookedly across his nose and his cheek flattened on his work. She stepped into the light, then turned and looked behind her. There were no rocks, no river, and no one who could possibly have spoken to her. The hall, dimly lit now the door was open, was just as it usually was. As Flora shut the door behind her she couldn't help shuddering.

"Why are you still up?" she cried, and her own voice sounded so loud and accusing in the silent house that she glanced around as if someone else had spoken, startled all over again.

Lionel's eyes opened slowly. He stared ahead of him blankly, then felt his nearby books with one hand. Pushing himself upright, he sat there, blinking.

"How crazy!" he said. "I simply put my head down for a moment . . . What are *you* doing up, anyway?"

Then he looked at her more closely. "What's up, sweetheart?" he asked gently. "Aren't you feeling well?"

"I had a bad dream . . . " Flora said. "At least, it must have been a bad dream, but it went on after I woke up."

"Lucky you to be able to tell when you're awake and when you're asleep," said Lionel. "I'm not too sure which I am, right this moment."

" . . . so I thought I'd have something to eat," Flora finished lightly. The thought of food seemed more reassuring than ever.

"Of course! That's the right thing to do," Lionel agreed. "What shall we have?"

Flora looked behind her at the door and thought of the hall behind it, shadowy but unmistakable.

"Biscuits?" suggested Lionel, taking off his glasses and rubbing the bridge of his nose. There was a red dent in one side of it.

"Then we'd have to brush our teeth and the pipes would clank," Flora said. Fear subsides slowly. She felt completely awake and ready—even anxious—for conversation. She went into the kitchen and found an imported summer apple, not nearly as crisp as apples from their own trees, but entirely free of codling moth. There, in the kitchen, she glanced casually down at the knuckles of her right hand and saw they were rough and gray. She had scraped and bruised them, but there was nothing except her memory and good sense to say she had not done it on the wooden panels of the hall.

"Dad," she began, coming out through the bead curtain. "I really do think this house is haunted."

She expected him to make a joke of it, to roll his eyes and pretend to glance nervously over his shoulder, but perhaps the early hours of the morning were not good times for joking about ghosts. Lionel looked up and around the walls, at the pipes shrouded in lagging, at the curious colored embroidery of the electric wiring running over sturdy rough-seasoned joists, braced against one another. Something about his expression astonished her.

"Do *you* think so, too?" she cried, but Lionel refused to meet her gaze. "I don't mean that it's haunted by anything wicked," she added hastily. "Just something that—you know—sort of keeps an eye on us."

"If it's haunted by anyone," Lionel said, "it's haunted by my old man, and he wouldn't hurt any of us."

"Still . . . a ghost!" said Flora.

"When I began the alterations I used to hear him shouting at me as I pulled nails out," Lionel remarked reminiscently. "You know how they groan. So sometimes I think he hammered bits of himself into the house when he added on to it, and now he can't tear himself away."

Flora though of her grandfather.

"He used to be crabby with me," she recalled.

"He was so used to getting his own way," Lionel told her. "But he was a wonderful father. And he was a wonderful doctor. Everyone said so. There are people still around to this day who owe their lives to him."

"What else?" asked Flora.

"Isn't that enough?" asked Lionel. "Being a doctor and saving lives?"

"Was he good *fun?*" Flora asked. "Did he make jokes?"

"Not the way I do," answered Lionel, sounding a little melancholy.

"I'd rather have you," Flora said quickly. Lionel looked pleased and surprised.

"Would you?" he asked. "I couldn't cure a common cold. Of course, I could always get you a tax exemption."

"I meant as a father, not a doctor," Flora said.

"Thank you for those kind words, Flora," Lionel replied. "I shall always treasure them."

Flora opened the door and looked into the hall. It was just as usual, but she found she could not bear to walk into it on her own.

"I'll escort you to your door, Madam," Lionel said, crooking his arm gallantly. Flora hesitated, then hooked her arm through his. As they stepped into the hall she spoke in a whispering rush.

"I thought I was in a cave," she whispered rapidly. "Well,

it felt like a cave . . . there were rocks all round me. I banged my hand."

Her story came out sounding like a midnight game. The only words in which she could describe what had happened to her were the words of a fairy tale. Yet her hand, holding the apple, was still somehow remembering the feel of the rocks. She breathed in and out, but only she could tell she was breathing a different air from the breath she had taken a few minutes earlier in the hall.

"I think this house really is haunted," she repeated stubbornly. "Dad, sometimes I see a boy watching us, and I think it might be Grandfather's ghost, guarding the house." She always called Lionel "Dad" when she wanted him to take her seriously, and in a way he did take her seriously now, but not seriously enough.

He put his arm lightly around her and, as she leaned against him, sighing with relief, he said, "Go to bed, honey. That's where you belong at this hour in the night. And remember this. Even if old Lionel is prowling around the house still, he'd never hurt you. He'd be a kind ghost."

"Even if we change the house?" Flora asked. Lionel looked around the hall.

"We haven't changed it much, have we?" he whispered. "Anyhow, it isn't his house anymore." But he did not sound completely certain of this.

"It won't be our house until we've got the walls all finished and the new windows and things," Flora whispered back.

"Don't you start in on me," Lionel sighed. "I'll do it when I have time."

And he opened her bedroom door for her.

Flora dived into her room, leaped into bed, and burrowed under her blankets again. Even though the apple was not crisp, it was sweet, and it comforted her as she lay there nibbling at it, wondering what had woken her up, and who had spoken to her in the hall, and why a house which felt like home in so many ways could also feel so untrustworthy, so full of other people's dangerous spaces.

Chapter 8

OVER THE EDGE of the stone shelf there suddenly appeared a pair of feet in old-fashioned school shoes, and gray socks with a red stripe around the top. Where the socks left off, a pair of scratched knees began. And then a whole boy swung down over the wavering weatherworn edge, hanging by his fingertips, wagging in the air like a clumsy flag, before he let go. He stretched out like an X (arms up, legs out) as he tumbled almost on top of Anthea. Staggering, he quickly recovered and pulled himself to his full height.

He was shorter than she, and younger too—perhaps nine years old—an angular boy, with a pointed face, bright blue eyes, his hair falling onto his wide forehead in a series of sandy commas. It was the boy of her first dream, the owner of the stereoscope, the child in the photograph on the wall in Lionel's room. Anthea felt she had been told his name, and had a vague memory that something sad had happened to him, but all that was in another place. Here, she mainly remembered him waiting for her as she pulled herself up out of the crack in the world. Laughing, he scooped up the crayon, as if it were definitely his.

"What are you doing here?" he asked abruptly. "I wasn't waiting for *you*."

"Why were you hiding?" she asked in reply, and his blue eyes slipped away from hers.

"Just being careful," he answered. "Who *are* you? How did you get here?"

"I'm Anthea," Anthea said. "Don't you remember helping me up through the crack in the world? I dream my way here."

A bright crafty smile flickered across his face. He began to dance a little on the spot, jiggling from one foot to the other, pushing his hands deep into his pockets.

"Dreaming!" he exclaimed in a light childish voice. "How can you be? This is *real*."

He had already begun moving forward down the road, almost as if he were trying to dance away from her. But as he went he looked back over his shoulder, inviting her to join him. Anthea hurried after, surprised to find how pleased— how *relieved*—she was to have company, even though this boy was too young to be a proper friend.

"Isn't anyone else coming with you?" he asked. "Someone else on the road back there? Another boy? Older . . . black bushy hair . . . green eyes . . . bossy?"

"No," Anthea replied. "There was only me . . . and now, you."

"I'm the main one," he said, sounding pleased with himself, but looking puzzled, even dissatisfied, as well.

They moved along side by side, glancing slyly at each other when they thought such glances would not be noticed.

"I followed the arrows," Anthea said at last.

"They were private arrows for someone else," he told her.

"Private arrows on a public road," Anthea pointed out.

"This is a private country, though," he said. "The road's mine. The mountains, too!"

Anthea did not want to argue with him.

"I'm only here for the space," she said peacefully.

"It folds out of nothing, this space does," he cried, flinging up his arms. "I invented everything in it."

"Invent a way out of this gully then," Anthea said challengingly. She was tired of the gully. Sometimes she thought she heard it closing quietly behind her, as if it were being zipped up when she wasn't looking. She felt she didn't have quite enough air in her lungs and breathed in deeply.

"It doesn't work like that," the boy answered. "Once you've invented something you can't just change it. It sets."

"It looks set," Anthea agreed, thumping the rocks on her right. "Set but faded."

For it did seem to her that though she walked down out of the whiteness into a colored world, the colors were softer and paler than they were in the place where Flora lived, that place where she waited in between dreams.

"Faded!" cried the boy indignantly, looking at the rocky walls with a mixture of alarm and affection. "It's not faded. It's Viridian. It's just funny that *you* should be here, that's all."

"I think I come here because there's plenty of room here," Anthea explained. "It's very crowded where I come from."

"It was crowded for me before I came here," the boy said. "Leo took up all the space there was."

"I have a cousin who takes up all the space, too," Anthea replied sympathetically, half guessing who Leo might be.

The road and the river curved together, giving each other plenty of room to turn. Around the curve in the road Anthea saw the end of the canyon. Ahead of them the rocks opened out and the road burst into sunshine once more. Anthea found her fear of a few minutes ago had completely gone. She looked out over a green world of open slopes set with bouquets of dark trees, and then turned happily to look at her new companion. He was dressed for wandering in a long jacket and a wide belt which jangled with many objects . . . a Swiss army knife, a tin cup, a flat metal bottle, a soft leather bag closed by a drawstring. On his wrist he was wearing a bracelet similar to the one she had found in the stereoscope's box.

"I've got a bracelet like yours," she said. Holding out her wrist to show him the sunburn she saw with surprise that she was actually wearing the copper bracelet itself, though she had put it back in its box and had put the box on the bottom shelf in the spare room.

"It isn't a *bracelet*," he cried. "It's a vambrace. Leo made it for me. When I wear it no enemy can cut off my right hand."

"What enemy?" Anthea asked, startled, looking around the empty world.

"You have to be ready—just in case," he said. "See that cloud?"

He nodded toward a cloud . . . the same lolloping grayish-brownish cloud she had seen when she first set foot on the road, a cloud which rose up out of the land rather than floating down from the sky.

"That's the battle," he said gloomily. "It shifts around. Suddenly you can be in the middle of it, for no reason."

"It's been going on for days now," Anthea said, and he nodded.

"It goes on and on forever," he said somberly. "It never stops." Then he smiled and laughed, as if he had made a joke.

Anthea shrugged and walked a step or two forward, but he didn't follow her. Something about the sight of the battle troubled him.

"Come on. Look at all the space just waiting," she encouraged him.

"Perhaps I ought to wait for Leo," he said. "He'll be along soon."

"Leo, the bossy brother?" asked Anthea.

"Yes," he said. "That's his Viridian name."

"Viridian!" Anthea repeated aloud, looking around. She had called it Viridian to herself, but hearing someone else say the name several times meant that she was in a known place. She even believed the outlines before her grew darker and more confident as she said it. "What's *your* name?"

"I'll give you a clue." He began his jiggling dance, glad

to change the subject. "I'm a fabulous beast: a little bit eagle, a little bit lion."

"I don't know," Anthea replied. "A sort of dragon?"

"Griff," he said. "Short for Griffyn. I don't use my other name—not here."

But Anthea was glancing past the battle smoke toward the water and the dragonish island rising up out of it. She knew that Griff was looking at it, too.

"Is that a lake over there?" she asked.

He looked at her incredulously. "Don't you know anything?" he cried. "That's the sea. It's in the heart of things, and the island is in the heart of the heart. That's where I want to go. But I have to be careful. I might walk straight into the battle."

Anthea felt very brave.

"I *thought* it might be the sea," she said. "I'm going there, too. Really going! And if I come to the battle I'll just walk around it. There's plenty of room."

She wanted him to come. The last bit of the road had been more fun with a companion. Nevertheless, she marched on a few steps ahead of him without turning around, and after a few seconds heard his footsteps following her, just as, earlier, she had followed him. She turned to speak to him, but somehow the air thickened and tangled her. Startled, she fought back only to find herself caught between familiar sheets. She was waking in her bed. Griff had vanished and with him Viridian and all its wonderful space. Through the hole in the wall Flora was watching her.

Chapter 9

"I HAVE A LOVELY SURPRISE for you," said Molly on the following Monday when Flora and Anthea got home after school. "We're going to garden."

"Oh!" groaned Flora, clapping her hands over her head and pulling a series of terrible faces. "Do we *have* to?"

"We do!" Molly declared. "There's a special sale at Cleland's Nursery. I've ordered the trees already. All we've got to do is collect them, pack them on to the roof rack, drive home very carefully, and plant them behind the rose garden—you know—on that weedy triangular piece between the roses and the creek. And after that we can leave everything to nature."

"Collecting and planting is just about everything," wailed Flora.

"Well, while you've been lounging around at school, dilly-dallying with math and so on, Teddy and I've been digging holes for trees," Molly said. "I've dug and I've carried buckets of compost and rotted pine needles. All *you* have to do is to help me tie the trees on to the roof rack, then help me untie them, and *then* hold them straight while I shovel the earth around them. So stop all that fussing!"

"What will we water them with?" asked Anthea, thinking of Molly's strict rules about wasting water in the summertime when there was no rain to fill the tanks. She and Flora had to shower together, huddling under a feeble sprinkle that seemed almost too tired to bother falling on them. But low water pressure was just another thing she had to put up with until nightfall, when she would sink into bed, yawning and secretly pushing her hand under the pillow to find the Viridian notebook.

Falling asleep over the weekend, she had immediately found the road under her feet, while Griff danced on ahead, though always glancing back at her, making sure she was following him. Sometimes there were slopes to climb; sometimes they lost sight of the sea until the next rise in the land enabled them to look out across a beautiful countryside, the familiar gleam of water, and the island waiting for them.

All Monday, with the voices of other children chattering around her, in the school playground and on the bus, Anthea had wondered, "What am I doing here?" And then she wondered just where "here" was.

She was glad to have Griff's company, but he was younger than she, bright but boastful, looking at the trees and grasses of Viridian and saying, over and over again, "I invented all this. Everything here's mine." "I'm only here for the space," she would reply, though there did not seem to be as much space now that she had come down from the mountains. Yet she had chosen to come down, and in the end she had wished for company. *Beware*, her grandfather's painted gaze seemed to say as she walked under it. You might get what you think you want. And sometimes she intercepted a strange intent stare from Flora, who knew something was going on and probably wanted to be part of it. But Anthea hugged her secret space to her heart, asking about water and looking innocently at Molly who was saying, "I did a huge wash today. I've saved buckets and buckets of water."

They climbed on to the verandah to find three buckets, two watering cans, a preserving pan, and a bright blue plastic container, all lined up. They were brimful with water which had previously been through the washing machine and was now waiting to be carried out to the holes Molly had dug behind the house.

"Other people don't have buckets of dead water on their sundecks," Flora complained. She was right. The water looked quite dead—gray and exhausted—with a soapy scum around its edges.

"Other people don't have a chance to plant forests," said Molly. "In a year or two we'll have a little woodland there, and we'll be able to picnic under the trees. And then a few years after *that* we'll say, 'Remember the day we planted those trees. This forest wouldn't be here except for us.' "

"And then . . . " asked Anthea, liking these ideas.

"Oh, well, one night we'll probably see strange things coming out of it—magical green people, unicorns . . . "

"Forestry trucks!" Flora interrupted her. "Hey, listen! What comes out of the forest on sixteen legs?" Nobody knew.

"Snow White and the seven dwarfs!" she cried triumphantly, and added, "it isn't the best time of year for planting a forest, is it?"

"If it were, we wouldn't be getting these trees so cheaply," Molly said. "They're a bargain. Now everyone out to the car!"

Lionel's car was the grand one of the family, shiny inside as well as out. On weekends he polished it carefully and locked it in the garage with the good door so that the hens could not perch on it. Molly's car, an old Volkswagen beetle, stayed outside in all weathers. Hens perched on it, and Taffeta slept either in its shadow or on its warm roof, depending on the weather. She was underneath it today.

"She'll run away when the engine starts," Molly said, but Flora insisted on shifting her, just to be on the safe side. Glorious watched smugly from the verandah rail, a safe, indoor cat who didn't have to scurry under cars to find a bit of shade.

They all crowded in, and drove slowly and noisily along the little bays that the sea had eaten out of the hillsides to the nursery where the trees were waiting for them. They were done up in bundles of five, each bundle fluttering with little orange labels saying *Cleland's Nursery*. When they actually saw the trees, Flora and Anthea both became more interested in the idea of planting a forest, for the trees, though spindly, were quite tall.

"Instant forest," Flora declared.

"Just add water!" added Anthea, and they laughed to-gether for the third time in a week. Teddy watched them as they helped Molly hoist the bundles of trees on to the roof rack.

"It's like Christmas," Flora said. "We always put the Christmas tree on this roof rack and drive home singing." She began to sing to the tune of "Jingle Bells" in a squeaky voice.

"Planting trees, planting trees, planting all the day, mak-ing instant forest so the bank won't fall away!"

Anthea looked at her with interest. Flora had suddenly reminded her of Griff dancing on the spot, but Flora at least did not think she owned the world. Indeed, she was anxious to share it. Anthea joined in singing, too, tugging down on the cords which Molly flung across to her from the other side of the car. She and Flora sang together as they drove home, with Teddy joining in with a song of his own, and when they grew silent at last, Molly began to talk. She talked about trees, saying that she had always wanted to live on the edge of a wood because trees had wonderful powers. They had an an-cient architecture, could draw water up three hundred feet into the air to refresh their top leaves, and could change sun-shine into food for themselves and for the animals and insects that ate their leaves. They had a dark phase and a light phase; they could outlive man and break stone, taking from the earth and giving back to it.

"Trees are magic. We're planting a whole forest of green magicians," she declared.

Anthea had imagined she would simply put up with the tree planting, working hard to tire herself out so that, later on, she would fall asleep immediately; but, unexpectedly, tree planting began to entertain her. She and Flora carried the water by putting a stick through the handle of the buckets which swung from side to side between them splashing a gray soapy water on to their sandals.

"Humpty Dumpty swung on a pole," sang Flora.

"Humpty Dumpty was poured in a hole."

Anthea joined in. As they sang, Molly tenderly spread out the roots of the trees. Anthea and Flora took turns to hold them straight, while Molly and whichever girl was not holding the trees packed soil around the thin trunks. Zeppelin wandered in and out, smelling each tree.

"Don't pee on those trees, Zep!" cried Flora. "Give them a chance."

"Yes," cried Anthea. "How would you like it if you'd just been planted, and a dog full of puppies came and peed on you?"

Zeppelin smiled, a smile full of white teeth and red tongue, a smile with a soft black edge. Then she lay down and began to roll around as if rolling in warm dirt were an exquisite luxury. The rooster came and scratched at the edge of the wood, calling the hens when he thought he had unearthed something delicious. Even Taffeta helped to garden, digging holes of her own which she then covered in. Or she stalked the laces of Teddy's sneakers, which, having come untied, followed him like tame pink worms as he went solemnly from hole to hole—squatting and peering into each of them until he found one he liked. Then he climbed into it and held up his arms as if he too wanted to be planted.

"Plant Teddy," suggested Anthea, pretending to water him with an empty watering can, and he screamed with excitement.

When they were finished, the forest (each tree planted far from any other) looked young and defenseless. The orange tags fluttered like small flags. Molly hammered stakes in beside the taller trees, then tied the trees securely to the stakes, with strips of rag torn from an old nappy.

"They're not in straight lines," Anthea remarked. "But that makes it more foresty."

"Nature is mostly jumbled up," Flora said to Anthea, inventing one of her sudden theories. "You've got to be careful of it or it goes into your head and jumbles everything you've got there." She hesitated, and then said in a troubled voice, "You know, last night I thought . . ." She stopped.

"What?" asked Anthea. It was a new feeling, being curious about Flora. Usually it was the other way around.

"It was quite spooky, really," said Flora. "I thought the hall was made of rock." She glanced, rather anxiously, at the knuckles of her right hand. Anthea, glancing too, saw a series of little scabs like the dotted line down the middle of the road.

"Dreaming?" Anthea asked, not altogether pleased to think Flora might be dreaming of other worlds, too.

"No," said Flora. "I was awake. I *had* dreamed something . . . I don't remember what . . . because I sort of jumped
myself awake. But after I'd woken up, I began touching stone
where there wasn't any, and hearing water."

"Water!" exclaimed Anthea.

"Water trickling down all around me . . . and a river flowing," Flora replied defensively. "But I can't have, really. Perhaps I'm going to be a mountaineer and my hand's just letting
me know what is in store for me. Perhaps it has the gift of
prophecy."

She looked down proudly at her hand, as if she might
read her fortune in the scabs on her knuckles.

"Lionel will be here soon," said Molly from behind them.
"I'd better make a gesture toward getting dinner ready."

Anthea looked up and saw that there were indeed late
shadows on the hill. More than two hours had gone by, and
she had not once longed for the road and Griff. All that time
she had been entertained, even happy. It seemed to her then
that she must have somehow carried some of the space of
Viridian back into the everyday world with her, but kept it in
her own head, in behind her eyes. Or perhaps there had
always been a magical space there which she had somehow
looked over or looked through until now. Viridian's spaces
might have helped her to see it for the first time. Yet she didn't
want to lose Viridian, with its silences and mysterious inner
sea. She longed for dinner and homework to be over so that
she could go to bed. She even refused to be interested when

Lionel got out his hammer and rule and a box of nails, and put on his carpenter's apron before sitting down to look quickly through the newspaper.

"He's actually going to *build*," Flora hissed to Molly.

"I think we've shamed him into it by planting the forest," Molly answered.

"I heard that. Don't think I didn't," Lionel called. "I'll just read the *For Sale* notices and then I'll get stuck into the walls."

Flora stared at him, her mouth slightly open, apparently waiting for him to start. Just as if nailing lining on walls was a magical trick, thought Anthea scornfully. It would take more than lining on walls to change this old house.

"Is it time for bed yet?" she asked, trying to yawn.

Flora rolled her eyes in Anthea's direction. Her gaze was sharp, but somehow distracted as if something else were occupying her real attention. "Molly said she'd read to us. Don't you want a story?"

"I'm tired after planting that forest," Anthea replied, smiling past Flora toward the island bathed in sunshine which was waiting on the other side of sleep.

Flora saw the smile and knew Anthea was being mysterious about something, but she could not worry about it too much for she had a mystery of her own. On the irregular wall behind Lionel, the dark skin of his shadow flowed in and out of the bare joists, and beside it flowed a shadow that was not his.

"Do you see anything there?" she asked Anthea, pointing. Anthea, barely bothering to look, yawned and said she didn't.

"I'm too tired to see extra shadows," she told Flora. "I must go to sleep."

But as it happened, it was Lionel who went to sleep, falling sideways in his chair with his hammer and nails set out, expectant but useless, in front of him.

Chapter 10

EVERY NIGHT, before going to sleep, Anthea carefully touched the notebook under her pillow to carry her through into Viridian. On Monday night it worked, just as it had worked before. But her first feelings were that she was somehow out of breath, and that fingernails, not her own, were scraping across her palms. She found she was scrambling up a hillside, holding on to handfuls of the dried grasses that grew along a track, rough but distinct beneath her feet. Anthea understood with surprise that the road she had come to know so well had taken a more difficult form. It was surprising, too, to feel a sharp pain in her side, as if she had been climbing like this for a long time. She paused, and pushed the hair out of her eyes and squinted up the slope to where Griff, a few feet above her, was looking impatiently back over his shoulder. When their eyes met he immediately gave his slanting smile and beckoned her on. Beyond him was the hilltop, and beyond that a great storm cloud. They were climbing toward bad weather.

"How much further do we have to go?" called Anthea, longing to stop and catch her breath. Up until now, uphill or downhill, she had somehow floated along.

"Up and over," Griff exclaimed restlessly, looking toward the hilltop. "That's all."

"What's happened to the road?"

"Oh, well," Griff paused. "It just dwindled. I suppose I must have stopped thinking about it." His voice was casual but he looked down at the track under their feet with uneasy puzzlement.

It was late in the day in Viridian. Though they were facing toward the storm clouds the sun was still falling pleasantly on their backs. Anthea caught up with Griff, and they scrambled on, side by side. Anthea felt that he could easily have swarmed away from her but that, for some reason of his own which was nothing to do with friendship, he did not want to leave her behind.

"How long before we actually reach this island?" she asked, and that was new, too. Until now it had always seemed that there was plenty of time, but suddenly she was impatient to be there . . . *to get it over and done with*, she thought to herself, and was immediately ashamed of the thought.

"On the other side of the hill," he promised, coaxing her on. "Maybe!" he added. Until now, he had been lighthearted, sure she would follow him. Yet, now he was watchful under his brightness, anxious to draw her on if she showed any sign of hesitation.

"Let's stop for a moment," Anthea said. "There isn't enough air."

"There's plenty," Griff cried. "Plenty!"

But when Anthea stopped, he stopped, too. He did not want to go on without her.

"Rest when we get to the top," he bargained.

"No. Now!" she said, deliberately sitting down and turning her back on the hilltop as she stared back the way they had come. The colors were still soft and faded, but many little sounds she had not noticed rushed in at her. She could hear her first companion, the wind, of course. But now thin meadow grasses stirred, and hidden insects called to one another in tiny clinking voices. From her feet the track stretched back down the slope and joined the wider road skirting the hill, or undulated back across other smaller hills, back through the canyon, and then up sharper slopes into the mountains, so white and so far away. In the end it vanished into the snow, yet Anthea, looking higher and higher, believed she saw points of light flash, disappear, and flash again, and remembered the hall with the spinning mosaic, the keyhole doors and the weeping stone.

"Come *on!*" Griff pestered her, but Anthea lay back on the grass and closed her eyes, enjoying the hot sunshine on her eyelids and the smell of the grass, a little like the smell of hay, but with a greenness about it.

"I dreamed I planted a forest," she said, puzzled. "Well, I think I dreamed it. Where does this road go to? Tell me again?"

"To the island," said Griff.

"Yes, I know, but what *is* the island?" she asked, wondering why she had never asked before. "I mean, does it have a name?"

It was a simple question but she felt all Viridian hold its breath and wait for the answer.

"It has lots of names," Griff replied in a small, reluctant voice. "Mostly people don't talk about it, but everyone has to go there in the end."

"Why don't they talk about it?" Anthea asked, opening her eyes wide.

Griff went on talking, but without answering her question. "Leo was supposed to come with me, but I ran on ahead and he's never caught up with me . . . I waited and waited. I'm sick of waiting. That's why I sent for you. I know that now."

The breeze blowing across Anthea's face suddenly felt chilly. She sat up sharply. She did not like the feeling that she was there only because Griff had sent for her.

"Now I half want to go back," she admitted.

He had been standing behind her, staring up at the top of the hill, but at her words he plumped down on the grass beside her.

"No going back!" he cried. "You *wanted* to come. No giving in."

"Well . . ." said Anthea, "if the island's just over the hill . . ."

They began to climb again, and at last they stood on the

hilltop, side by side. Far in the distance, and still well below
them, the inland sea reflected the storm, but the island looked
warm and sunlit even though it floated on such dark water.
If she had had a telescope Anthea believed she might even
have been able to make out two slender, golden-brown people
diving and swimming through the sunny water. It was just
the sort of place her parents might have swum to. By now
she felt as if her parents had always been beautiful merpeople,
only accidentally on land, always arguing and making up,
bound to return to the sea one day and leave her behind. In
spite of Griff's luring promises, the island was still far away.

At her feet the land stepped down, down, and down, in
a series of vast terraces. At some time in the distant past a
round valley had been cleared and then lined with fitted stone
and turned into a gigantic theater. Thousands of people must
have filled it once, but now she and dancing Griff were the
only audience.

They had scrambled into the wide U-shaped embrace of
a fallen arch, though there were other such arches still standing, refusing to crumble gracefully. Going under one, she saw
she could walk down a wide stair to find a place in one of the
rows of seats that curved all the way around the theater,
descending to what looked from here like a small level paved
space; but which was really a stage—an arena—and an arena
invaded at one end by forest.

For the old theater had been taken over by trees. Huge
stones had been thrust aside, mortar fractured, whole slabs
tilted at odd angles. Up through the cracks hundreds of sap-

lings were erupting eagerly toward the light, shattering the stone as they grew. The first trees must have looked like ghostly intruders in the empty theater, but as they grew they had made it their own. Anthea was looking into a forest haunted by the memory of an ancient ruin, rather than a ruin overgrown with trees.

"Oh, we're only up to the coliseum," Griff said, and sighed. (*Shove it in with the ancient monuments,* said Flora's voice from over a week in the past.) Stung by this odd memory, Anthea shook her head. What was she *doing* here, standing at the point where the live wood invaded the old stone? Behind her, Griff shook his head, too, bewildered and then suddenly angry.

"What have you done to it?"

"Nothing," said Anthea. "How could I?"

"These trees shouldn't be here," he said. "Look at them, breaking everything up!"

"They're alive," Anthea said, liking the forest more than the coliseums. "I like live things." As she said this she saw the deep summer colors around her begin to blister, as if they were merely painted on and the sun was too hot for them. The song of the grasshoppers changed its pitch, went out of tune; the solid stone grew glassy, the trees around her seemed to stiffen and straighten, and eerily, the naked walls of her bedroom wall began to show through them. Anthea knew she was waking up. Griff knew it, too.

"Come back!" he commanded. He did not move, but Anthea felt as if he had somehow seized hold of her and dragged her back toward him. The stone lost its transparency. The trees fell back into more graceful shapes.

"What did you do?" she asked him in surprise, horribly alarmed to find herself seized in that way.

"What did *you* do?" he said, still sounding angry, but interested as well. "How did you make those trees grow through stone? You said you'd planted a forest."

"Yes, but not here," Anthea replied.

"It doesn't belong in this space," Griff answered, and Anthea once again recalled a card with two photographs on it, saw her own hand sliding it into a wire frame, felt herself looking through a mask and seeing space where no space could be. Griff was right. There had been no trees in the photographs, no roots like serpents twisting and pushing the blocks of stone further apart.

"You can just get out of here and take your forest with you!" Griff cried in fury.

"You're the one who stopped me!" Anthea snapped, hurt because until now she had loved this nonexistent space. "Perhaps I'm getting tired of Viridian," she said, surprising herself. "Perhaps I don't want to dream anymore."

But Griff's jiggling dance grew more and more agitated.

"I didn't mean it," he cried desperately. "Don't leave me here!"

"Well, you wake up, too," Anthea suggested.

Griff stared at her so furiously that she stepped back from him. "You'll be sorry if I do," he said. "I'll stand beside you and breathe on you, and then you'll be sorry."

Anthea tried to wake up, but felt the dream settling down around her. The faint colors deepened a little. "I've had enough for tonight," she thought to herself and wondered how she could pull herself out of Viridian in spite of Griff. She needed a strong hand to hold on to, something to tie her thoughts to, and the first person she thought of was Flora who was, after all, just through the hole in the wall.

Chapter 11

FLORA HAD THE HABIT of sleeping with her head under the pillow instead of on it. Nevertheless, she woke with her head echoing to an urgent voice which had spoken right into her ear.

"What's wrong?" she asked, sitting up, blinking and dazed, turning to look through the hole in the wall. But Anthea's bed was empty.

"Where are you?" she cried softly, but there was no answer.

Four nights had gone by, since, going in search of food and comfort, she had felt cold stone where there should have been polished wood, and smelled wild outside air where there should have been the inside scent of furniture polish. The room was so full of light that she thought it must be morning. It was the light of a full moon, licking the walls with tongues of cold silver. Flora waited, but Anthea did not return.

At last Flora hauled herself out of bed and saw, in a long mirror propped against the wall, her moonlit reflection also getting out of bed. It was too dark to see all the details. She shook her head sadly as she groped her way through the hole in the wall to feel Anthea's pillow and sheets in a businesslike way.

Anthea's sheets were cold so she hadn't just got up to go to the lavatory. Flora stood there, pushing her fingers through her hair, wondering what to do next. For a horrid moment she thought she saw Anthea, hanging limp and soft on the back of the door, but it was only her rose-colored dressing-gown with the velvet collar. Flora relaxed, then started again as something tapped softly at the window. Whirling around, she half expected to see a strange pale face, all red eyes and fangs, flattened against the glass. Instead, she saw her own reflection once more, but dark and half-transparent this time, swimming on the surface of the window. Something throbbed where she thought her heart might be . . . a moth fluttering against the window pane. Flora began to turn away, then spun back again. Out in the night, there on the other side of her reflection, she had glimpsed something impossible—a for-est—not the young, uncertain forest with the orange labels which she and Molly and Anthea had planted earlier in the day, but an *old* forest. There it was, out in the night . . . trees, trees, trees. And winding in and out of the trees was a pale, living slither, Anthea sleepwalking, floating along in the lovely sprigged nightgown with pin-tucks down the front . . . so pretty . . . so delicate.

("I'll just have to iron this," Molly had once said, though she hated ironing anything that was merely slept in. She had certainly never ever looked at Flora's striped pajamas with that half-smiling wistful expression.)

Flora scrambled back into her room, turned on the light, pushed her door open, and peered apprehensively into the hall. Four days had gone by, but it would be a long time before she would be able to walk boldly through her bedroom door without checking the hall first. The price of a magical life is lightheartedness. But tonight the hall was only itself. Flora sighed with relief, then stopped and looked again. On the moss-green carpet someone had drawn an arrow. The arrow head was the shape of a pointed oval with a black slot drawn across it. She thought it blinked at her, but in fact she was the one who had blinked.

"That Anthea!" whispered Flora, pretending to herself that this arrow was Anthea's work, though she knew very well that Anthea would never have drawn on Molly's hall carpet. Besides, Flora recognized this arrow. It had been drawn on the cover of the notebook that lived in the box with the stereoscope: dead Henry's childish tales of the magical land of Viridian. Flora wondered if, somehow, on the day that she and Anthea had sat by the rickety table on the verandah peering at the stereoscope pictures, some trace of Viridian had somehow seeped out like a stain to taint old Lionel's house. She looked sternly up into the painted eyes of her grandfather's picture.

"Huh! Ghosts!" she muttered, walking straight along the arrow toward the big room, letting anything that might be listening know that she was not afraid. "I'm not scared." Yet she *was* afraid, and hoped that her father might be working late, not on the wall . . . she didn't expect that, and anyhow there was no hammering . . . but on his accounts, perhaps, just as he had worked last Thursday night. If he were there, either yawning and grumbling, his trusty calculator in hand, or slumped over the table, accidentally asleep, she would be able to tell him that Anthea was sleepwalking, and *he* would say, "You get into bed, sweetheart, and leave it all to me."

But tonight the big room was dark. Lionel's green pack and his brown office case sat side by side on one end of the table, looking like opposites, yet still belonging together. Flora edged past them, opened the back door, and slid out onto the verandah. A warm summer wind rushed around her, trying to swirl her pajamas. Pajamas couldn't swirl, but the wind wasn't disappointed. It stayed with her, light, free, and friendly.

The verandah ran around three sides of the house. It always creaked and cracked underfoot, so Flora felt her way down the steps and walked on the path between wallflowers and the kitchen herbs, until she was facing the forest. Once outside, she was engulfed in the curious light of the moon, silver and leaden at the same time. Looking down to make sure she did not stumble over any of Teddy's toys, or step on the sharp bones that Zeppelin carelessly left lying around, she saw another arrow drawn on the side of the house and pointing her forward. Something moved beside her . . . only a cat . . . her own Taffeta, enjoying the prospect of a midnight moonlight walk with one of the people of the house. Flora picked her up, and Taffeta started purring wildly, bunting Flora's chin so vigorously that Flora's teeth clicked together. At the same time another cat came from nowhere, running on ahead of them in short bursts, then waiting for them to catch up before running on again. Glorious was enjoying the night, too. Taffeta craned her neck, staring in outrage at the newcomer, but she did not stop purring, or struggle to leap away. Flora advanced with Taffeta in her arms, Glorious running a little ahead of her.

There was something odd about the forest. From inside the house it had looked like the first forest of the world. Out here, Flora found it was hard to tell just how high the trees really were. Those directly in front of her seemed no taller than they had been when she had held them upright for Molly that afternoon, whereas those at the edge, the ones seen from the corner of her eye, looked tall and old. Yet, when she turned and confronted them, they, too, dwindled into mere saplings, while the middle of the forest grew ancient and tall, its trees spreading out their arms toward each other, holding hands as if they might begin a dance the moment her back was turned.

Flora stopped. There was someone standing among them, apparently staring into a twisted puzzle of shadows where even a full moon could not shine.

"Anthea," Flora hissed. If she named this shape with Anthea's name it might turn out to be Anthea, after all.

But the figure turned, and it was black, not white. As it turned, Taffeta leaped from her arms, while Glorious hissed and arched her back. Both cats scattered into the night.

"You!" Flora said. She was sure this shadowy boy would not, could not, harm her, though he was not part of the natural world anymore. He was nothing now but ashes buried under a sweet-smelling old-fashioned white rose.

The face was somehow smudged, as if its colors had run together. The lips moved, but his voice could not be heard. He was holding out a hand that looked more like a shapeless paw, blacker than blackness.

Flora hesitated, then thrust out her own hand fiercely, shuddering as she did so. It was taken in a strange clasp . . . fingers not claws, but fingers of smoke. The scent of old-fashioned roses came out of the night.

Nevertheless, as the smoky fingers closed over hers, everything grew clearer. It was no brighter than it had been before, but now she was part of another world, part of Anthea's dream. Before she looked at the dream, however, Flora looked at the boy beside her.

He was about thirteen, a little taller than she was, with bushy hair like her father's, and a pale long face. Although she could not make out the color of his eyes, she knew they must be green.

"Where's Anthea?" she asked abruptly, and the boy turned his head.

"Over there," he answered in a faint far-off voice. "In a dangerous space. In dangerous company."

Flora found she was standing on the rim of a circle of ruined stone. Beside her was part of a wall with an arch in it, a wall carved with faces that smiled and wept stone tears. Such ruins did not belong to Flora's land where, in the distant past, houses had always been built of wood or woven of reeds. Something was tricking her mind into believing in space where no space existed, and filling the space with stereoscope pictures of old stone.

Both space and stone were pierced by hundreds of trees. Flora could smell the leaves—new, growing leaves, and dead ones, decaying richly underfoot. Between the trunks she could make out a shape she recognized, for she was looking into the coliseum of the stereoscope cards, but it was broken and tilted by the green power of the forest.

Anthea stood on the opposite rim, her nightdress swirling around her, face to face with someone shorter than she was, someone who danced on the spot, waving his arms excitedly.

"Who's that?" Flora asked. The boy beside her sighed and did not answer directly.

"We lost each other," he said. "He needs company to finish his journey." A strange idea came into Flora's head.

"Is it dead Henry?" she asked, her eyes growing round, her voice beginning to whisper.

"He calls himself Griff in Viridian," her companion replied carefully, as if there were only a limited number of words he was able to use. Flora felt him struggle, concentrating hard in order to have a shape and to talk at all.

"She *wanted* to go," he said. "But he'll take her to the island and there's no way back. You have to go through."

"Through what?" Flora asked.

"The hole in the middle of the zero," said the ghost beside her.

"Why don't *you* go?" Flora suggested boldly.

"But who'll look after the house?" he asked her in a hushed uneasy wail. "We have to protect our spaces."

House, house, house, whispered the forest around them. *Space, space, space.*

"It's our space now," Flora exclaimed. "We're allowed to change it. *You* changed it when you wanted to." She thought she could still feel the smoky fingers around hers, but when she turned to challenge the boy, to tell him that no one had the right to own a space forever, he had vanished. Flora knew she would have to find her way around the rim all by herself. She began working herself up to be brave. Actually, she thought, she wasn't doing too badly.

"I know where we are!" she muttered to the empty air. "We're inside the stereoscope. We're shut in the box. We can break our way out. Easy-peasy!"

The fingers she could still feel began to drift out through her own. Something moved ahead of her. A cat leaped from one stone to another, then paused as a second cat darted ahead of it like a friendly imp. Flora had company, and from here she could not tell one cat from the other. On moonlit nights, all moving cats are made of shadow. She began to scramble between the trees and the tilted blocks of stone. They felt cold and somehow soapy underfoot. Running and scrambling, Flora moved around one of the curving ledges where people had once sat watching the performances below. But the remains of the coliseum stretched themselves into infinity. The cold of the stone struck up through her feet and ankles, and Flora could not fight her way any further into Anthea's dream.

At last she stopped, shivering, even though she had been running so hard, even though the stars overhead were the summer stars of the southern hemisphere. Beside her, a big tree stood which had shouldered a whole flight of stairs to one side. An orange banner flapped from its lower branches. With her ghost-given night-sight Flora could see the words *Cleland's Nursery* printed on it. And a curious thing happened. She could feel the tree working, almost as if she had become the tree itself, doing all the things Molly had talked about during the afternoon: lifting water up through the channels of its trunk, busy in the dark altering the energy of daylight it had gathered into sugars the tree would be able to live on. *Photosynthesis*, Molly had said (as if the scientific word were as magical as *abracadabra*). Plants do it, and everything lives by it. Flora was standing beside a green magician with the power to transform worlds, a magician who was silently altering the air around them.

And now Flora remembered that when she and her friends were small they had played a game called *Tiggy tiggy touchwood*. When you touched wood you were safe. In the kitchen at home, when Molly wanted to avert bad luck, she laughed and touched the wooden mantelpiece.

"Photosynthesis," Flora said aloud, fixing her eyes on Anthea and laying her hand on the living tree. There was a tremor like an earthquake. Something bony twitched under the world's skin. All the angles and lines around her fell into disorder. Some things dwindled; others shot up into the air. The scent of roses came toward her on the playful wind, and broken stone rings became nothing but patches of broken light stretching across the garden and the fields beyond.

Anthea stood only a few yards away in the middle of the newly planted forest, staring into the empty night. The two cats crouched at her feet. "Walking in her sleep!" thought Flora. "Trust her! A beautiful orphan with long fair hair and a pin-tucked nightdress, walking in her sleep! It is too much." All the same she took Anthea's hand, which seized hers so desperately it hurt. Anthea was gasping quietly, dreaming, perhaps of swimming or of being on a mountaintop where the air was thin.

Flora was careful not to speak to her cousin in case she came out of her dream so suddenly that she died of shock (which everyone knew could happen with sleepwalkers). It was Anthea who spoke first.

"Where is he?" Her voice was puzzled and dream-ridden.

"There's only me," Flora said, leading her away from the forest. Anthea's hand tightened again as if it were glad to feel the touch of human fingers. "How did you make him let me go?" she asked, and then said, "Have I been dreaming? Where are we?" She was properly awake now and astonished to find Flora leading her through the night.

"You've been sleepwalking," Flora told her. "Shall I make us a cup of tea? Herb tea?" she added, thinking it sounded healthier for a sleepwalker.

Though the unlined walls of the kitchen looked as if they were full of little cupboards and crannies where anything might be hiding, it was nice to be there, safe inside, protected by the smell of last night's dinner, mixed with the faint smell of old smoke—a homely spell to keep darkness at bay.

"Were you dreaming?" Flora asked. "Cracks in the ground and an ironed wind?"

Anthea's smile faded. She saw Flora darting glances at her as she plugged in, first the little heater and then the kettle, longing to be told all about it. Of course she deserved to be told. But Anthea didn't want to tell. It was dangerous—she knew that now—but still it was something of her own in a house where there was so little space for her, so little space that everything private was precious and had to be guarded. Flora watched and waited, not sure if Anthea was struggling to speak, or simply trying to remember. But then she looked as if she *had* remembered and had decided to say nothing.

"No . . . " Anthea said. "No dreams . . . at least . . ."

Flora began warming the teapot, swishing the hot water energetically from side to side.

"Gee, you look a mess," she said with satisfaction.

But Anthea ignored her, looking around at the kitchen as if she had never seen it before. Beyond the bead curtain in the big room, Lionel's brown office case and green pack sat side by side on the table, somehow managing to get on together. Anthea was surprised to find how comforting it all was. No way out. I suppose I'm going to have to get used to living here, she thought, and felt the space behind her eyes, which she had first felt earlier in the day, stretch itself and grow a little larger.

But she didn't tell any of that to Flora.

Chapter 12

"GUESS WHAT?" said Molly when they came out much later in the morning, both feeling worn and crotchety, walking close together, but looking away from each other. Night memories were like memories of a strange play which they had acted out for one another.

"Something good?" Flora asked. "It had better be!"

"Yep!" said Molly, smiling to herself, and Anthea suddenly guessed.

"Puppies!" she shouted, astonished to find how much she had been looking forward to the puppies without quite letting herself know.

"Puppies!" agreed Molly. "Four of them. In the laundry. Now, hang on a minute . . ." But Flora and Anthea were scrambling for the laundry. Molly followed them, shouting that they were to be quiet and gentle and not worry Zeppelin.

Zeppelin's box, lined with pieces of an old tartan rug, seemed to be full of nothing but Zeppelin, tenderly licking her side. But it was puppies she was licking, four puppies crowded into one puppyish lump, and all cuddled against her. She smiled at Flora and Anthea, flattening her ears and flapping her tail a few times.

"Clever Zeppelin!" Anthea exclaimed. "Clever, clever dog! Hey, I think the poodle must be their father, don't you?"

"Aren't they *ugly!*" Flora cried. She had seen very young puppies before, but was astonished all over again at their tails and delicate ears, at the shiny softness of their new coats, at the pads on their paws and their squashed-up faces. Her amazement was so strong it felt exactly like happiness.

"You'll hurt her feelings," Anthea said, fussing Zeppelin. Flora gently picked up a puppy which immediately began squeaking. Zeppelin stood up anxiously so that the other puppies rolled over and began crying, too.

"She's a good mother," said Anthea admiringly. Teddy came waddling in behind them.

"Mine!" he cried, pointing to the puppies.

"Zeppy's!" Flora told him sternly.

"Until we find new homes for them," Molly called from the door. "Put them down. Give Zeppelin a little bit of time with her babies."

That morning everything went well. Anthea not only helped with the dishes, but helped to carry the mash to the hens. When the rooster started sparring with her she bravely waved the mash bowl at him and, since he was not feeling as serious as he sometimes did, he ran off clucking throatily, ruffling his feathers. Flora and Anthea both laughed at the same time at the same thing.

Then they went to look over the pig-pen fence at Minnie and Merlin the pigs.

"Lionel said we'd have pigs so that we could have bacon," Flora remarked. "We were going to be self-sufficient, but now we like the pigs too much to kill them. Probably he has to do extra work at night to keep two pigs happy."

"You wouldn't really want them killed, would you?" Anthea asked.

"No, but I wouldn't mind us being real farmers, not pretend ones," Flora said, sounding resigned. "I reckon you can be really self-sufficient and kind to pigs, too."

"We could eat them if there was an atomic war, and all the supermarkets blew up," Anthea suggested.

"Then they'd be radioactive," Flora said. "Anyhow, Lionel would probably bring them into the house to keep them safe. And the hens and the rooster, as well."

Anthea watched Merlin crunching a heel of stale bread.

"Will we have to give the pups away?" she asked thoughtfully.

"Yes," said Flora. "One dog is enough, and Zeppelin's not a real dog. I mean not a real *working* dog. Real farmers don't fuss their dogs except when they're in the dog trials on television."

"I'm a given-away pup," Anthea remarked after a pause.

"Given to a good home, though," Flora said quickly. The

shadow of a grin showed at the corner of Anthea's mouth, but Flora couldn't be quite sure what it meant.

It was a pity that after such a peaceful beginning the rest of the day turned out to be so angry.

They had left Molly in a good mood but now, when she came out through the bead curtain, she made it rattle like hail.

"*Don't* leave the mash bowl on the table," she cried crossly.

Anthea smiled politely and did her sliding-out-of-the-room trick.

"Where's Lionel?" Flora asked, knowing that something always went wrong the moment *she* was not there to keep an eye on things.

"He's made his morning escape, the coward," snapped Molly, "and left us all behind him in this dump. As usual!"

"Mum," Flora whispered, anxious to say something that she thought was very important. "Anthea said she was a given-away pup."

"He's brushing himself down on the hill pretending he comes from a reasonable house," Molly cried, not listening.

"A given-away pup!" Flora insisted.

"Not *more* puppies, not at this hour in the morning," Molly said half-cross, half-pleading. "The drain's blocked. The loo's overflowing. That wretched Teddy has probably been dropping things down it again. I *loathe* Tuesdays!"

"I said she'd been given to a *good* home," Flora added quickly, thinking of Anthea, and not of the blocked drain.

"I'll do something about it all *later*. Don't miss the bus," said Molly, thinking of the drain, not Anthea.

But Flora thought about being a given-away pup all day.

When they got home that afternoon, the drain was cleared, but Molly, who smelled strongly of disinfectant, was still cross. Flora didn't bother to ask her how many biscuits they could take. She tactfully collected a generous supply and went to join Anthea beside the puppies. They argued in a friendly way about possible names for them, but it was hard to tell them apart at this stage.

"Gelert's a good name for a dog," said Anthea, remembering a story she had once read with a noble dog in it. "Mind you, I don't think Gelert was a poodle."

"Gelert," repeated Flora, liking the name. "Suppose we call them all Gelert until we can tell which is which. Okay. That's enough puppies! Let's walk."

They set off along the track that ran out on to the little peninsula that was part of their land—Wakefield's Point, as it was named on maps. They walked in silence at first, watched by heavy shy young cattle with white faces and sparse white eyelashes.

"Our family has lived here from time immemorial," said Flora. She meant they had been there for about a hundred years. "Yours, too, because of your father. *You're* part of it."

Anthea tested this idea. To her surprise she found she did feel a little bit as if her ancestors had lived there from time immemorial. She could remember coming to the farm as a small child, could just remember old Lionel holding her up to look out over the harbor. It was *her* place, too. She was beginning to smile and agree, rather shyly, like someone who had refused to see something that was just common sense, when suddenly everything changed. Perhaps in stereoscope space and time, the storm clouds had covered the sun so that the sunlight, falling on the peninsula where Griff must have played as a child, had to darken in sympathy. The sky stayed cloudless, yet the light on the hills became wilder, fiercer— and suddenly everything, every single thing she looked at, had a singularity about it that frightened her. Her ears filled with a chorus of savage voices saying, "Now! Now! Now!" and "This! This! This!" "Look at *me!*" shrieked every blade of grass, every grain of earth. She tried to move out of this fear-some zone. "No!" said the air as if it were denying itself to her. Looking up, she saw Griff standing only a few feet away, his eyes fixed on her. He was in her world and yet he was still in Viridian, too. He was not just an image. He looked alive, yet his whole figure was consumed with a minute fe-rocious writhing, as if the atoms that made him were about to fly apart. The sea breeze blew Anthea's hair one way, but another wind from another land blew the commas of Griff's sandy hair in another. Once out of Viridian, Griff was trans-formed into a demon.

"Was there anyone in the family ever called Griff?" she found herself asking, trying to think of him as one of his own inventions, but Griff, drawing power from his name, was able to come even closer.

"Dead Henry!" Flora replied looking at her sideways. "Henry Griffyn. Old Lionel sometimes got mixed up and called him Griff. It's in that old notebook he used to write in."

Griff was only a few feet away. Anthea refused to look at him. She would refuse to think of him anymore for he had threatened to breathe on her, and she knew that if she felt his breath on her cheek it would be cold . . . as cold as death.

A moment later they reached the end of the peninsula and looked out toward the island. "That island looks a bit griffinish to me," said Flora knowingly.

"More like a dragon," Anthea replied, and Flora felt hurt, resenting her tight, cold voice.

The grassy land ended inches away from their feet. The peninsula fell away in a series of little cliffs. Far below, those sea gulls that still had chicks to care for were flying out from their nesting ledges over the sea, crying out, warning one another of the approach of strangers. Sea gulls, thought Anthea, concentrating. Sea, sky, space. By following Griff's road and dancing his dance she had linked herself to him. Now she must put him out of her mind . . . must break free. But before she could really begin to forget, Flora said a shocking thing.

"You *dream* of him, don't you?" was what Flora said.

"Are you mad?" Anthea said stiffly. "Dream of . . . of dead Henry?" She dared not give him his Viridian name.

"You do," Flora declared. "I know, because I see the other one . . . old Lionel. I'm beginning to work it out. Dead Henry's ghost has been waiting somewhere for Lionel to catch up with him, but Lionel's ghost won't leave the house, so dead Henry has chosen you instead. You can tell me because I believe it. Nobody else will."

Anthea refused to look toward the point where Griff had been standing a moment ago. Something cold stirred against her cheek . . . A damp sea breeze? a chilly breath?

"Are you crazy?" she said scornfully. "There's no such thing as *ghosts*."

Once again there was that odd quiver underfoot, the shrug, Flora had called it. To Anthea it felt as if the earth was swallowing something. Flora and Anthea banged their shoulders together, then sprang back from the edge and from each other. Before their eyes, part of the edge on which they had been standing only a fraction of a second earlier, broke loose, coming to pieces in midair. Separate stones curved outward toward the sea, frantic to be free from this terrible haunted boundary.

"An earthquake," Anthea said stupidly, but Flora grabbed her arm and pulled her back still further.

"How did you *do* that?" she asked.

"I didn't," Anthea cried indignantly.

"Those stones could fall on the baby sea gulls," Flora scolded her. "Are you turning yourself into a sort of poltergeist?"

"No!" Anthea screamed. "Just leave me alone, Flora Wakefield." For it seemed to her, though she dared not look, that Griff must be standing right beside her. She felt a chilly breath on her neck. Her long hair hung still, though the breeze was ruffling Flora's. "I don't want you talking about me. Talk about something else. Talk about the puppies instead."

There was another fall of earth and stones. Dust rose lazily from the cliffs below. It was amazing how much noise the rattling stones made on the edge of the still harbor.

Flora hung her head, but not in shame. She watched the loosened pebbles leaping and plunging, leaping and plunging, until at last they vanished, leaving distant white pinpricks on the green water. She seemed to understand something.

"Let's go back before you wreck the whole place," she said in a disagreeable voice. "You must hate absolutely everything about us."

"I hate all of the *mess*," Anthea cried, as furious as Flora, but much more frightened. "You have holes in the walls and hens making messes all over the verandah, and buckets of yucky awful scraps in the kitchen."

"Well, real things just *are* messy," Flora cried back.

"Not in a proper home," Anthea answered. "Real can be nice." Suddenly she forgot about Griff, for things that had been secretly thought for weeks were being said aloud. She and Flora were having a quarrel at last, and the quarrel was truer than Griff or Viridian could ever be.

"We were all right, and then we had to have you!" Flora shouted.

"And I had to come here and live in a pulled-down house with pigs and hens," Anthea answered. "I didn't want to. It's horrible."

Flora, walking ahead, came to a standstill so sharply that Anthea almost ran into her.

"Well, it must have been great at your *nice* house," she said, "because everyone knows your parents argued all the time. Everyone thought they might get divorced. Everyone *worried*." She moved on a step, and then turned back with the face of a cruel fury. "Everyone said they shouldn't have had children. They just went on that boat to get away from you. You lot were all *nice* but you couldn't be *real*." She stalked on a few steps, then turned and glared at Anthea again. "I was beginning to *like* you," she cried, and began to run as if compelled to put as big a distance as possible between them.

Anthea watched her go and, as she watched, felt the sea breeze lift her hair and cool her sweating neck. Slowly, she turned and looked back toward the edge of the peninsula. The demon Griff had vanished, if indeed he had ever really been there. Ahead of her, Flora leaped and ran—back toward the old house, with its roof that Lionel had paid for but not yet painted. Anthea chose another track from the various tracks that wove backward and forward across the hillside. Just as she had come to believe that there really was a space for her here, it had vanished again. She thought of Griff but only in an absentminded way, as if he were indeed a ghost, but a brittle ghost, an old story, crumbling at the edges. She began to run, too.

Anthea and Flora headed for home from different directions. They met like strangers at the wooden gate, which they climbed in silence, Flora hoisting herself over the end with the hinges in the proper way, Anthea scrambling at the head of the gate beside the loop of wire that tied it to the fence. They came into the house side by side, shoulder to shoulder, but further apart than they had ever been in their lives.

"BED!" said Molly later that evening, after a silent, awkward meal with nobody talking.

However, Anthea curled up more tightly in her chair, turning her shoulder a little way from the room, while Flora, lying on the floor, stared down into her book just as if she were really reading the story in it, and could not bear to stop.

"Time for your evening nap, darling," Molly said to Lionel, but her teasing words sounded sharp and strange.

"Don't go on at me!" Lionel said pleadingly. "I mean well. I was *tired* last night."

"You always *mean* well," Molly cried.

"I promise I'll do it on the weekend without fail," Lionel answered, standing up and trying to put his arms around her. "I'll even take time off work tomorrow so I can get started. And I'm sorry I said you smelled of disinfectant. Anyhow, I *like* disinfectant."

But she stepped out of his embrace, looking contemptuously along the naked joists, seeing shells and the teapot from a doll's tea-set, a tumbler filled with pencils that all needed sharpening, and ball-point pens that didn't work anymore but somehow had never quite been thrown away. There was a tin lid filled with drawing pins and rubber bands, and a pair of false teeth made of red and white plastic which ran across the floor clacking greedily when they were wound up.

"Remember the day when you said it would only be the work of a weekend or two to line all this?" she asked. "That was before Teddy was born."

"Are you saying I don't work hard enough?" Lionel asked her. He was beginning to shout.

"No," Molly cried back. "But I'm saying you never have time to do anything here, and it's partly because you don't want to. You feel too guilty about changing it around."

"Look, I want to get it finished as much as you do," Lionel cried, "but there are things that have to be done first . . . things that have to be *paid* for."

". . . the roof," said Molly wearily. "The foundations!"

"Yes," said Lionel. "As a matter of fact, yes! The house is sagging at the nor'-west corner. It needs repiling. *You* know that as well as I do."

But Molly marched past him through the rattling bead curtain.

"Women!" said Lionel, looking from Anthea to Flora.

Anthea refused to notice him, and Flora returned his gaze so sternly that he followed Molly through the bead curtain, and they could hear them hissing at one another on the other side. Suddenly, Lionel roared despairingly.

"Do you think *I* like seeing you unblocking drains and feeding pigs and planting forests?"

"Do you think I really mind?" asked Molly, sounding gentler. "I love it a lot of the time, but just sometimes I'd like things to be . . . to be *beautiful*. I mean, here we are in this lovely place and . . ."

"I've had it!" Lionel declared. "Let's sell the place. Let's go back over the hill. Let's go *out* some evenings, even if it's just going to the pictures. Let's have a *nice* house. I could pay for home-help rather than foundations and roofing iron."

"You don't mean that!" Molly sounded shocked.

"Oh, but I do," Lionel told her. Then he stamped out through the bead curtain like a man striding through a storm. He did not look at Flora or Anthea this time. His footsteps sounded on the verandah and then he was gone.

"What a day of fights," Flora said aloud. "*Us* fighting! *Them* fighting!" It was the beginning of an apology.

"I've heard much worse fights than that," Anthea replied. Then she got up and went out into the hall. Flora heard the door of her bedroom close, and thought how funny it was that someone with a hole in the wall should still go to the trouble of closing a door. She went to the kitchen doorway and peeped, almost shyly, through the bead curtain.

Out in the kitchen Molly was checking the seals on half a dozen jars of tomatoes she had bottled during the day. Five of them had sealed tightly but one would have to be done all over again. Molly looked tightly sealed herself.

"Mum," said Flora.

"Hello, sausage," Molly said, using an old pet name for Flora, one which she had liked when she was little but hated now. It showed that Molly was not really thinking of what she was saying.

Flora wanted to tell her mother that she was worried about Anthea, and that at the same time she wanted Anthea turned out of the house, given to someone else. She wanted to try to tell Molly about the stones leaping away at the edge of the peninsula and to confess that she had said terrible things to an orphan.

"Mum," she whispered. "I think we're a doomed family."

Molly only laughed, though not very cheerfully. "Dear heart, what rubbish!" she said. "We're like all families. Blood must flow!"

"Why must it?" Flora asked.

Molly shrugged. "Happy things happen and sad things happen," she said. "Old Lionel died, but then Teddy was born. Anthea lost her parents but other good things will happen . . ."

"I *know* that," Flora cried, frustrated at being comforted with the wrong sort of arguments, but not sure what the right ones were.

"Well, what is it then?" Molly asked, sounding puzzled, too, and a little hurt at Flora rejecting her explanations.

"I said awful things to her," Flora explained. "But she said them, too. We both did."

Molly turned back to her jars of tomatoes. "She probably didn't mean them," she said, but not as if she believed it.

"Yes, she did!" Flora declared. "We both did. I think she's under a spell. . . . Dead Henry's got her."

"You see, no one realizes just how much work there is in a natural life," Molly said. She was talking to herself rather than to Flora. "That's why so many people like *un*natural lives. I mean they may sneer at the 'rat race,' but rats have it easy. For real slog, day in, day out, give me the natural life and a natural family. You'd better try and *deserve* these tomatoes."

Then she turned on the electric kettle and began to sort out a new seal for her reluctant jar. "It's going to be overcooked, but who cares! I'll write *Overcooked* on the label, and we'll use it in soup."

The words of Flora's worries dissolved like grains of bitter salt on her tongue.

"Sweetie, you *must* go to bed," Molly said, turning from the stove to put her arms around Flora and giving her a bear hug. "Don't worry about your old man and me. We're all right, really. Just a few cross words between good friends."

"Maybe you should have a holiday together," Flora mumbled. ("Go sailing!" she nearly said.)

"When Teddy's old we might," Molly said. "When he goes to university, say. Something to look forward to." Then they hugged and patted each other on the back, comforting one another for something without knowing quite what it was.

"I'll think about Anthea," Molly promised. "And now, Floradora . . . bed!" And this time she said it in the voice of someone who knew what she was talking about.

Chapter 13

ANTHEA, who did not want to dream ever again, was curled in her chair trying to think of a way to stay up all night, but in the end she went to bed. The fighting drove her there.

It was true her own parents had often argued, shouting cruel things at one another, but they made their quarrels up quickly, hugging each other in a way that shut Anthea out. She had often felt she was not so much their child, a true *part* of them, as a precious possession, no more than the car, or her mother's rings. But when Molly and Lionel began to fight that evening Anthea found herself more upset than she could explain to herself. She wondered if there was something about her, a sort of radiation, say, which forced people to shout and fight and abuse each other and cry when they came too close to her.

"I'll go to bed but not to sleep," she thought, slipping between the sheets, refusing to look through the hole in the wall into Flora's space. "I'll stay awake until I get back to being ordinary in ordinary life. I'll make myself *glad* to be here."

At first there was no problem in staying awake. She lay on her back staring up into the dark, a thousand thoughts churning around inside her . . . a thousand almost-thoughts. For they were more like pieces of broken pictures mixed together and slowly boiling around, mind-soup made up of scraps that rose and sank and turned over and over. One piece came to the surface and then vanished as another replaced it . . . puppies, and pig buckets, tin masks with the power of creating magical spaces, and, at last, her parents, not frozen as they were in the photographs beside her bed, but moving freely, coming toward her, smiling and suntanned, then walking right through her, making for an island where they would sail and swim and be golden and happy: nice, not real. But then other swelling pictures pushed them aside. She saw the hens fluffing out their feathers, each standing on one leg and giving little throaty clucks to other hens. She saw the rooster scratching with active sideways scrapes of his yellow claws, but then the rooster dissolved into the ruined theater which formed and faded in turn as the pigs, thrilled to be fed, came trotting, snouts raised, through the slow tumble of her thoughts.

Flora came into her room and got ready for bed in a crisp silence. Anthea could feel Flora planning to say something to her, and then deliberately not speaking. She felt Flora's back being carefully turned on her, remembered the unkind things they had said to one another, and understood that when, panic-stricken by Griff's writhing presence, she had shouted how dirty the house was, it was an Anthea of two or three months ago who was shouting through her. The Anthea of today didn't want to lose the hens or the puppies, or even the pig buckets; was frightened, too, of losing Flora's funny songs. She wondered how she could ever explain to Flora how dangerous it had seemed to talk about dead Henry and old Lionel while dead Henry, whose Viridian name was Griff, was breathing on her, forcing his way out of nonexistent space into her everyday life, just as she had forced her way from everyday life into his nonexistent space against all rules. Perhaps she, in her own way, was as fierce and possessive as Flora. However, she was sure of one thing . . . in this everyday life she must never make way for dead Henry.

How easily Flora went to sleep! Perhaps Anthea herself drowsed a little, though her eyes stayed wide open.

Suddenly, she was aware that there was a narrow band of light lying across the sheet only inches from her nose. At first, she thought it might be coming up through that old crack in the world, that she and her bed were going to be sucked up by imaginary space. Then she realized it was nothing but light from the hall. The band widened. Someone was opening the door and looking in at her.

"Oh, it's only you," she whispered in relief.

"Who were you expecting?" Molly whispered back. She came in and glanced sideways through the hole in the wall.

"Sound asleep!" she said. "But not you?"

"I can't sleep," Anthea said, secretly meaning that she wouldn't.

"I could feel someone was awake," Molly murmured.

Then she sat down on the edge of Anthea's bed, bent over Anthea, and kissed her cheek.

Anthea sat up, wanting desperately to be hugged by Molly. She had always enjoyed Molly's hugs in the past when Molly was just an aunt. Now she was more than an aunt but not quite a mother, and Anthea did not know exactly how to hug someone who (if things were to be fair) must really belong to Flora and Teddy.

"Anthea, don't stick out your elbows when I hug you," Molly said. "Now! Hug me again."

"You don't *have* to hug me," Anthea muttered.

Molly still held her.

"Anthea, I want *you* to hug *me*," she said. "*I* want to be the hugged one."

So Anthea did the hugging, and found herself weeping soundlessly on Molly's shoulder, and her tears, pushing their way out through a veil of stone, began dissolving the veil away.

"I get so cross and tired at times," Molly told Anthea, "but I try not to let Flora know. She's got to think I'm as good as possible."

"I said awful things to Flora today," Anthea told Molly. "I said this was a dirty, untidy place and that I hated it. Well, not that I actually *hated* it, but almost."

Molly said nothing, still letting Anthea hug her.

"She said I could get out and go somewhere else," Anthea went on. "But I can't. There's nowhere else that wants me."

"I know you must miss your own place," Molly said. "I

still feel jealous when I remember how comfortable it must have been."

"There was only me to look after, no baby and no pets," Anthea said. "Mummy and Daddy used to get tired, too, because they both worked. Mrs. Harrow used to come and do the cleaning. No hens!" Anthea and Molly giggled a bit, thinking of the sundeck. "Then they went away without me, to be on their own together. I think they'd been fighting, but not . . . I mean, they just wanted to be together."

"Everyone fights," Molly said. "But they'd have got over it. Look at Lionel and me! I truly want the sort of life I've chosen, but at the same time I can't help wanting it to be perfect, too."

"It's hard to have children if both parents work," Anthea went on, "it's best to have someone at home." She paused, and then went on, almost against her will. "But—suppose they've just pretended to drown and secretly swum off somewhere, away from me."

Molly drew back from her, peering through the darkness. "Anthea!" she exclaimed softly. "That's such nonsense. I remember how much your parents wanted to have a baby. Gosh, when you were born your mother said to me, 'I thought I wanted a boy, but the moment I saw her I knew she was the one I had wanted all along.' They didn't swim away. They just drowned. Drowned."

"If I'd been there I might have rescued them," Anthea muttered feebly.

"If you'd been there you would have drowned, too," Molly said. "The people who owned that boat didn't have proper lifebelts and stuff. You *know* that. Everyone told you. It was in the papers and on television."

Anthea had been told this, but for the first time she believed it, and understood the difference between knowing and believing. For months she had obstinately struggled to force two pieces of a puzzle together when they didn't want to go. Now, Molly had given one piece half a turn and perhaps she herself, unknowingly, had already half-turned the receiving piece. Behold . . . they slipped effortlessly together and made a pattern, sad but peaceful, as natural as a forest.

"Anthea, it was sad . . . so sad . . ." said Molly, "but, darling heart, you simply must . . . not *forget*, but just think of the next thing. Anthea, Lionel and I don't forget your parents, but we do feel really *lucky* to have you."

Anthea pressed her nose against Molly's neck and smelled disinfectant. Then she said in a tiny, tight, mumbling voice, "But I can't be the *best* one to you. Not really best."

"Right this moment you *are* the best one," Molly whispered. "You're the best one now because you *need* to be best."

The whispering might have got into Flora's dreams. She tossed restlessly under her blankets.

"Shhh!" said Molly. "Don't wake her. This is just you and me, being best to each other for a while."

Though Molly was next to her and Flora was only a few feet away, Anthea found there was plenty of space around her . . . not the nonexistent space of the stereoscope where the colors were faded and the wind refused to blow on her. This space was real, and it was all her own.

"Flora can have a turn at being best tomorrow," she said quickly, feeling generous because she was so comforted herself.

"Turn and turn about is fair," Molly agreed. "Different people being best at different times."

She and Anthea held one another, saying nothing, and after a while Anthea forgot that she must stay awake. She let her eyes close once, twice, and then a third time. Feeling her grow limp, hearing her breathe differently, Molly edged her back on to her pillows.

Anthea murmured protestingly but did not wake. She slept, and in her sleep her left hand closed around her right wrist and felt the copper bracelet rising up out of her skin, coming through her skin, become real under her horrified fingertips. A voice spoke to her from nonexistent space. "I've got you now," Griff said triumphantly. "We're going on, and this time we won't stop until we get there."

Chapter 14

DREAMING ONCE MORE, Anthea found herself in a terrible place where the air trembled and screamed, and everything around her flickered. In front of her stretched a dreadful, smoky space. Fires burned. She was one of a crowd of shadows. Featureless people, moving beside her in the gritty twilight on either side of the road, ran and shouted. Flames roared and cracked like whips in the windows and doorways of a burning house. The colors were faded, yet still powerful in their own way. The house burned, but there was no heat coming from it. In the beginning, Viridian had been almost nothing but space. Now, all spaces were being consumed. She breathed in, her lungs filled with smoke, and she choked and coughed. Someone tugged at her arm. It was Griff, staring frantically around him. "Why did you bring us *here?*" he cried.

"Where are we?" Anthea screamed back at him. Her words were snatched away by a gust of hot air that rolled out of the smoke, overwhelming them for a moment, then rolling on.

"The battle!" he shouted back. "I told you! It shifts around. It goes on forever."

In the dreadful light he looked as if he were made of wax. The sandy hair on his forehead stood out like dried blood.

"You said we'd follow the road," Anthea shouted back. "Where is it?"

He pointed down at their feet. They were ankle-deep in refuse, in mud and rust, and bits of metal, but between the fragments she could still make out the stones of the road.

Something thudded through the air overhead, striking the ground somewhere in front of them. There was an odd gulping sound, as if whatever it was was swallowing prey. Dirt sprayed up over them, and to her surprise Anthea felt it stinging her face and hands. An invisible force swept past her, lifting her hair around her. It was no more powerful than the gust of icy wind that had welcomed her when she stepped out of the hall at the beginning of the road. But after that first great breath on her face and hands she had felt neither hot nor cold, nor the movement of a breeze over her skin, until now. Something had changed. Anthea tried to imagine what Flora would have done in these circumstances. Anyone who could face up to the rooster would cope bravely with a battle.

"Let's get out of it . . ." she said in Flora's voice. "Run!"

Griff stood still, smiling his bright smile, but suddenly Anthea realized he was terrified. He had been terrified for every step of his invented road, though he had tried to hide his fear. He had danced on the spot and beckoned her on out of fear. Griff's bright smile was a sign of terror.

"I don't want to be swallowed up!" he cried. "Help me!"

Smoke billowed over them, and she lost sight of him, though he was only a step away. "Where are you?" he screamed. As the smoke thinned and his shape showed, as gray and featureless as the other shadows at first, she had an idea. Taking off her chain with its silver padlock, she quickly threaded it first under his bracelet and then under hers, so that, in Viridian at least, they were chained together. Then she linked her fingers with his. All the time she was saying to herself that nothing in this place could harm her, and that if she were safe Griff must be safe, too.

"You'll know I'm here, even in the smoke," she told him, gasping and coughing as she spoke.

When she moved, he began to move along with her, but very slowly. In the end, she tugged him mercilessly, until his legs began to run of their own accord. The road was there. Their feet were still on it, but it had become a crazy paving running through the very heart of the battlefield. Whole sections of it had cracked or subsided yet, dodging and leaping and stumbling, they managed to skirt the damage and then to find the road again. The things at Griff's belt wobbled and clanked against one another. Dust and dirt seemed to be as much part of air as earth. Once again something thudded and gulped. Once again, Anthea's hair lifted around her. Smoky figures rose up through the smoke on either side and curved out of sight into smoke that was even more dense. There was an immense concussion somewhere to the right, and a sound that seemed, not so much loud (though it was loud), as deep.

Its echoes went on and on, thrown back at them by the sky. Griff was jerked away from her. His feet actually left the ground. Their slippery fingers parted. Anthea felt a ferocious wrench on the arm that was linked to his, but the chain held, and she, not being entirely part of Viridian, and shielded in some way by the memory of Molly hugging her on the other side of sleep, was less affected by the explosion. Yet she did not escape altogether. Not only was her arm painfully twisted but the fabric of Griff's collar dragging across the bottom of her fingers actually burned her. As she felt pain, all the colors grew stronger and the noise grew louder as if she had shaken water out of her ears. Never had the nonexistent space seemed more real than it did at the moment when she did not want it anymore. She and Griff got to their knees, then to their feet, linked fingers again, and ran on.

Ahead of them the road suddenly broke up. There was a big hole in it into which they stumbled, sheltering gratefully behind its rough edges.

"Wait! Wait!" gasped Griff. "Just wait."

"Run!" commanded Anthea. "Run!" But she didn't mean it. To her dismay, she had begun not only to smell the smoke but to feel it—smearing, rough, and acrid—at the back of her throat. Where had it all gone—the wonderful space? She coughed and spluttered continually. "Run!" she insisted, hating the new gritty feel of each breath, and the terrifying roar that seemed to come at her from all directions. Griff crouched down, his bent knees as high as his chest. He bowed his head and hid his face in his hands. "Don't you want to get to the island?" Anthea asked, as severely as Flora might have done. He lifted his head at the thought of the distant lakes and the island.

"I'm frightened," he said at last.

"Of the battle?" she asked.

"Of the island," he wailed. "I'm too scared to go there alone."

Crouched in the hole, hearing the cries of the warring world around her, Anthea could not think of what to say next.

"Why?" she asked.

"You have to let go, and I want to hold on," Griff muttered, grinding his teeth.

"But you said it was good place to go to," she cried.

"You *wanted* to go," he pointed out. "It's good if you *want* to go there."

The smoke cleared above them. Anthea straightened and peered out of the hole. Only a few feet away something like a branching twig stuck out of the mud. But it was not a twig. It was a human hand.

"Run!" she commanded him, thinking she sounded more like Flora than ever. "No stopping!" And she set off without waiting for any argument and, being chained to her, Griff had to move, too.

So they scrambled out of their hole and ran, weaving and dodging through the smoke which somehow seemed to be rolling more and more thickly over the road, until they found themselves in the next hole.

"What *is* Viridian?" Anthea asked suddenly. She had

asked this before, but never quite as seriously as she asked it now.

"I told you." Griff was always ready to boast about Viridian. "Lionel—Leo, that is—was always telling me what to do, but I was the boss of the stereoscope and the place in it, so I made up the land of Viridian. I got the name from my paint box."

"It's a good name," Anthea agreed.

"Yes, but then something happened . . ." His voice wavered. "I don't remember what it was, but *I* got here and I've never been able to get out again. And Leo hasn't ever come looking for me."

"Well, where is he then?" asked Anthea. Then, remembering what Flora had told her, she thought she knew.

"Maybe he forgot me," Griff said.

"You have to do some things yourself," Anthea said. Just as she was getting over her own fear she found she was having to bear part of Griff's. It weighed heavily on her, but she willed herself to stand up. The damaged earth had taken on a rich, wet brownness, the smoke was a dirty gray, and, as color had come into things, the feeling that nothing in this dreadful place could touch her was deserting her.

They hauled themselves out of the filthy hole and now, through the drifting smoke, Anthea saw the road stretching before them almost as it had done in the beginning. She hesitated at last, besieged by dust and noise. Griff, who had taken the lead for the first time, tugged at the chain.

"Go on without me," Anthea said. "I want to wake up."

"No!" Griff said, and he actually began to jiggle on his toes. He was on the point of dancing again. "Someone has to watch me being brave. That's what makes it true."

Anthea knew just what he meant. They ran on. The smoke ahead of them thinned.

"We're almost through," said Griff, as if he could hardly believe it. But at that moment there was a great *whumping* sound. Anthea felt herself flung to the ground which immediately began to twist and crack. She leaped to her feet at once, dancing a dance of her own between the series of terrible smiles now opening in the road. She slipped and fell into one of them, fully expecting it to close its sharp lips over her, devouring her forever. However, if anything, it smiled more widely still and she was able to pull herself out again, using only one hand, cutting her palm so that she left a series of bloody handprints along the broken edge of the road.

Her other hand was held up in the air by the chain. A moment later, Griff's invisible fingers twisted in hers once more. He pulled, while she pushed herself in the direction of her chained hand, and behold, she was back on the road once more, with Griff at her side. They had come through the battlefield. They were safe on the other side.

In front of them stretched a curious landscape . . . ridges intersecting other ridges, making a grid whose hollows were filled with the most astonishing assortment of junk . . . worn-out machines, old prams, torn books, broken chairs and bicycles, pencil stubs, snapped crayons, washing machines for which you could no longer get spare parts, pianos with hopelessly cracked soundboards, burnt saucepans, teapots without lids, ballpoint pens that would not write any-more . . . all the junk of family life spread across the struts of the land. In the distance she could see people wandering in this desert, turning it over, all of them wearing puzzled and desolate expressions, all looking for something valuable which had been lost in the confusion. Suddenly, she thought she recognized someone. She thought she recognized Molly, with Teddy trailing behind her, picking her way through it all and shaking her head despairingly.

"I've got to get back," she cried.

"Look *this* way," Griff commanded, turning her around.

Anthea turned into the same icy wind which she remem-bered from long ago, but now she would feel it, and now she had to shrink from it. Underfoot ran the road, only a ghost of its wide well-maintained beginning, but still there, until a yard further on it ended in a jagged edge.

They were standing on the lip of a cliff. The battle and the rubbish dump were behind them. Ahead of them there was nothing but sky and sea, and the dragonish island per-petually bathed in sunlight. There was plenty of space, but Anthea could not use it anymore. She had to pant to get enough air, even though the smoke had cleared away.

"It's ended . . ." Anthea gasped stupidly.

"But we can see the rest of the way now," cried Griff joyously. "We might have to creep down the last bit, but we're almost there."

"I've got to go back, though," Anthea explained desperately, trying to turn away. She wanted to be certain that the woman she had seen was not Molly.

"But you've chained yourself to me," Griff pointed out. Then he smiled and took the padlock of the chain that tied them together and squeezed it between his finger and thumb. Anthea saw the catch bend, tugged wildly, and found the delicate chain had become as strong as steel. She and Griff were truly locked together. Dancing on the spot, Griff gestured toward the island.

"I'm not letting you go again," he cried. "This time there's no stopping until we get there."

Chapter 15

As FLORA BEGAN TO WAKE and saw moonlight angling through the window once more, she thought that the previous nights had leaked through into this one. She thought it was the same moonlight, and that she had to live through everything—through the stone hall and the deceptive melting forest—all over again. But this time she would do it better so that there would be no fights afterward. Then she woke properly, and remembered that outside, the moon would be just past full. The light in her looking glass was not quite the same moonlight as it had been the night before.

She heard a sound that reminded her vaguely of a bicycle tire being pumped up, and turned to look through the hole in the wall. Anthea was sound asleep, propped up on her pillows, arms straight down by her sides. She had the strange look that big dolls have at times, the look of being perfect but ghostly, their faces unchanging. But Anthea was doing something that dolls don't do. She was panting, making a hoarse, rattling sound. Flora thought of the things Anthea had said to her, and the things she had said back. She wondered if Lionel's and Molly's argument, and the fear of shifting to another home, were punishments she had to suffer because she had been unkind to an orphan. She felt certain that if Anthea did not wake up and forgive her at once, she would lie awake worrying that Lionel and Molly would go on quarreling, now they had learned how. She leaned toward the hole in the wall.

"Hey!" she said. "Hey, you!"

Anthea did not wake but Flora was not surprised. She was often slow to wake herself.

"Anthea!" she called. "It's me, Flora."

All the time she knew she would have to get out of bed, climb through the hole in the wall, and shake Anthea awake. If she spoke any louder she might wake Molly, who listened for Teddy even in her sleep. Muttering to herself, Flora scrambled through the hole in the wall and shook Anthea gently.

"Wake up just for a minute," she hissed.

But Anthea, smiling and panting, did not wake.

Flora stared down at her, trying to see what she really looked like in the dim moonlight reflected from the windowsill. She looked beautiful and lost, a very young sleeping beauty who might easily sleep a hundred years. Cautiously, Flora turned on the bedside light. As soon as she saw Anthea bathed in the yellow ordinary glow of a low-watt bulb she knew something was wrong. For one thing, Anthea's eyes were not properly closed. A gleaming crescent of eye showed between her eyelashes and her cheeks. And nobody was ever so *empty*, even in sleep. For a dreadful moment Flora thought Anthea might have died of unhappiness in her sleep, and that she, Flora, would never be forgiven. The thought of life without Anthea immediately became intolerable. She almost stopped breathing herself until she realized that of course Anthea, breathing rather noisily, was certainly alive. Flora gave a gasp of relief and began living once more. On the sheet beside Anthea's calm unconscious face was the print of a hand, bloodstained thumb and fingers, then another and another. Flora flipped her limp hand over and stared in consternation at the cuts across the palm which slowly oozed blood. She glanced down at the scars no bigger than freckles across her own knuckles. Then she shook her cousin again, this time desperately.

Anthea held up her arm as if she were showing Flora the time. The drops of blood fell on to the sheet. Her silver chain had somehow become tangled and taut around her wrist. It was cutting into her skin. But Flora was too anxious about the partly closed eyes and panting breath to bother about the chain. She leaped to the door. She was going to fetch Molly. But when she reached the hall, instead of going to her parents' room, she turned into the spare room, walked confidently through the dark, and felt for the box on the bottom shelf. It came easily toward her, curiously chilly between her hot hands. She opened it and felt for the square green tin with the golden printing. It seemed to be covered in frost.

As Flora took out the cards she touched the copper bracelet and understood it was conducting coldness from somewhere, but she did not stop to think about that. She took the stereoscope and the cards, half expecting to hear her grandfather saying, "Now don't touch, Flora!" in his grave, firm voice. She could feel him in the room as Leo.

"You can't let Anthea get lost," she said, without turning around. "Well, I'm not going to, anyway."

Then she carried the stereoscope and the pictures back to her own bed. Switching on her light she looked at the stereoscope critically. The door creaked slightly and she jumped wildly, clasping both hands over her mouth so that her scream would not be heard, but it was only Glorious oiling her way in, hoping to sleep on the end of someone's bed.

"I have to put everything right," Flora told the cat, pretending to fan her face with her hand, acting out the shock she was still feeling. She looked at picture after picture, trying to work out how to get into the space that formed there, time after time. "I'm going to fetch her back. She can just learn to live with the pig bucket whether she wants to or not. I have to live with it. She can, too."

Picture after picture sprang out in three dimensions. Views of gorges and mountains, museums and ruins, wars and mountaineers, and prospectors climbing the Golden Stair Trail, Chilkoot Pass, Alaska.

"I'm doing something wrong," she thought, staring in despair at the cards spread around her. "Why doesn't it work for me?" There was a slight thud at her window. She turned. Taffeta had leaped in from outside. The two cats looked at each other. Taffeta crouched. She spat at Glorious, but her heart wasn't in it any longer. After a moment she changed her mind and began washing her own back as if she had lost interest in any contest. Glorious picked her way through the hole in the wall, and leaped on to the end of Anthea's bed. If Anthea could use the stereoscope to get into Viridian, why couldn't Flora? The next picture was a statue, a veiled head. "Let me in," she commanded it, and though the head did not answer her, someone else did.

"Someone has to pull you through," breathed a voice at her elbow, and there he was—the ghost of the house, standing beside her, looking down at the pictures on the cards.

"All right! Pull me in, then!" demanded Flora. "Why do you waste time mucking around here, trying to stop your own family living their own lives in this house?"

"I built this house," he breathed, as if that explained everything. "Once, during a sad, doubtful time in my life, I built it up and out, and built myself with it. I built all doubt out of myself. You'd pull the house apart if I didn't guard it, and then there would be nothing left of me."

"There's not much left now . . . you're only a ghost," Flora told him. "I reckon you should be somewhere else doing something different. And anyhow, if you're such a good guardian why don't you stop dead Henry from pulling Anthea into stereoscope country?"

"It's an imaginary space," he said. "Dangerous! And I'm imaginary. If I go there I won't be able to get back again."

"What's the use of worrying about the shape of the rooms when the people of the house are giving up and getting ready to go," Flora cried. "Houses wear out! They have to be changed."

"Families change!" repeated the faint voice beside her. "Wood and tin keep their shape longer than flesh and bone."

Flora sent most of the cards flying off her bed with a sweep of her arm.

"*I'm* your true house," she cried fiercely, holding her arms wide so that he could take a good look at her. "Well, part of it. So's Anthea. Why go haunting wood and nails while the blood gets lost in nothing?"

"The blood!" He sighed and fell silent.

Without looking up, she knew he had gone, for suddenly there was Taffeta in bed beside her, pressing close to her and kneading with her front paws. She purred, but it was from anxiety, not contentedness.

"If at first you don't succeed . . ." said Flora stubbornly, sliding a picture into the stereoscope, and sticking out her tongue at the vanished ghost. Adjusting the card holder in its grooves she suddenly found the exact place where the picture became three-dimensional, but this time it was more than simply three-dimensional. This must have been the one scene that had been waiting for her, for it rushed toward her, a gaping mouth which swallowed her up in darkness and storm and the beating of horses' hoofs.

Flora found herself on a huge grassy plain, with a sharp wind striking into her face, ruffling her hair. It was evening. The sinking sun flooded the whole plain in an unearthly light—all the stranger because the sun was shining narrowly between the horizon and the rim of a rolling line of black clouds. Flora had never seen such a storm. The clouds were rounded, and for all their blackness were illuminated by the western light creeping in under them, so that their curves were both luminous and lurid. Flora had never seen threat and wonder so dissolved into each other. Looking down at her hands she saw her skin had the sinister glow of the storm, its freckles embedded in it like specks of gold. Her blue pajamas glowed. She, ordinary Flora, was transformed into a girl of precious metals and jewels, frightening and thrilling herself. For here she was in Viridian, but where was Anthea? How would she ever find her in this world of signs and space? She needed a sign that was just for her, or better still, a guide. A flight of birds passing overhead cried out in voices both harsh and musical, telling each other about the stranger on the plain below.

As she stood there, Flora felt the ground begin to shake in a way that reminded her of the quivering under the peninsula and of the stones leaping from the crumbling edge and escaping to the sea. But, somehow this was a different sort of shake . . . something steadier and more prolonged. A black mass was moving toward her. As it came nearer she felt the rhythm of its approach rising through the soles of her feet and trembling in her ankles and knees. Her whole body began to shake with it.

A herd of horses was galloping toward her. Lightning flashed across the black clouds and, when the thunder came, it was not so much a rumble as a violent crack of sound. Flora looked up, half expecting to see the sky ripped apart like an old sheet being torn into useful rags. She even forgot Anthea for a moment, for the horses with their streaming manes and tails, their wild hoofs and gleaming eyes, were so amazing, so beautiful and terrifying that, even though she believed she might be trodden down, she moved a step or two toward them.

Then she saw that there was somebody on the back of the first horse. It was a boy, half-naked, as wild as the horses, but oddly familiar. Looking directly at her, he flung up his arm and the horses wheeled away to the right—so close to her that she could see their yellow teeth when they curled their lips, could smell them, could feel grass and earth from their churning hoofs fly up against her cheeks.

They slowed, they circled. She became the center of a ring of horses. The lightning flashed again, running an instant livid hand across their hides. The boy was Leo, looking wilder and freer than he had ever looked before. His long-delayed journey had begun. Flora felt the wind tug the grasses, subside, then tug again.

"We have to go to the island," he cried to her, making a new voice for himself from the wind and the storm and the cry of the birds.

"Is it far to the island?" asked Flora.

"I know the way," called Leo, sounding both sad and triumphant.

The storm painted him briefly with light.

"I'm not a very good rider," Flora said humbly, as a small horse, black as jet, came up beside the other one.

"You'll be able to ride here," Leo said, but he dismounted and gave her a leg up, all the same. "Now, don't get too excited," he suddenly added in the grave voice of old Lionel. "Take things quietly, Flora!"

Flora sat on the horse, staring around at the grassy plain and the clouds and the crooked rod of light that fell across the sky once again. The echo of this single blow filled the air with a thousand crackling voices, all rushing together within a second to become one immense roar.

"To the island!" shouted Leo, sounding young again.

"To the island!" shouted Flora, and the herd of wild horses broke into a gallop, with Leo and Flora at the head, the rest of the herd streaming behind.

Sometimes it seemed to Flora the horses were racing almost as fast as time itself, and sometimes it seemed they were standing still. Sometimes the movement around them was the movement of the storm. Or perhaps it was the turning of the vast wheel of sky she glimpsed above her as the sun set.

Chapter 16

THE ROAD HAD DWINDLED to a track which sometimes crumbled into nothing. It zigzagged down the cliff, less a track than a series of dangerous ledges, and it seemed to Anthea that not only the road but the whole land of Viridian was coming apart. The road wasn't needed, of course, when they could see the lake in front of them. Anthea imagined that they must look like two children in an old-fashioned picture book, scrambling hand in hand down through a land filled with hidden fairies and magical beasts.

Griff was the only one consciously holding on. Her own hand hung limply, only a chain's length from his, but it felt as if it really belonged to someone else—some weaker, easily betrayed person—not the Anthea who, only a little over a week ago, had looked keenly and coldly into the stereoscope.

Griff inched downward confidently, angling his feet and testing footholds, pressing himself back toward the face of the cliff, bathed in the light of the setting sun. He looked like nothing more than a lively ten-year-old, enjoying a risky adventure. He breathed easily while Anthea gasped and panted. The sea and its island often seemed not like space, but like a painted wall, risen up only inches before her face and stealing air from her. There was almost no space left for her in Viridian, almost no space at all. She shuffled over a ledge so narrow it would not hold each foot completely. Her outer toes could feel that there was no stone under them. Then the track seemed to grow out under Griff's feet again. He slowed down so that Anthea could catch up with him, and they were able to walk, briefly, side by side.

"Leo says that when you get to the island you can rest for a little bit, light a campfire, or lie in the sun," Griff said suddenly. "But then you go *inward* . . . into the center, the smallest point. It's so tiny you couldn't even see it through a microscope, but it's there, and you go *through* it, you *squeeze* through, and then, when you come out on the other side . . ." He stopped. "I don't remember," he confessed in a confused voice. "Not quite."

"I thought you invented Viridian," Anthea gasped.

"Not the island," Griff admitted. "Well, not the part about the smallest point in the middle of it. Not the hole in the middle of the zero. Leo says that's always been there. There and not there, at the same time. Like the horizon."

But Anthea thought the horizon was definitely there, a curious line ruled in both water and light.

Then the track widened again, and now they could see it stretching on ahead, sloping downward to a band of trees which had been invisible from the top of the cliff. Beyond the trees they could see sand and shells. And then the sea, the island, and the sunset with black clouds billowing toward it.

"Run!" Griff cried. To him it looked like open space, but to Anthea it still looked like a picture painted on a stone wall, something she was about to smash into. Griff ran, tugging at her, pulling the chain, so that she had to pound down the slope after him, feeling the wind lift her hair and blow it out behind her. And though she shut her eyes and panted, she did not smash into anything. The wall moved grudgingly backward, making way but giving her as little space as possible.

They came down into a narrow woodland of birch trees still in full leaf, but with a tattered late-summer look to them. Indeed, they were just beginning to change color. The track ran into the fallen leaves which lay in drifts under the trees. Griff shouted as he ran. His shouting was almost a song.

"In the middle of the island there is a trapdoor, and through the trapdoor there is a stair, and the stair leads to a room, and there is a chair in the room . . ."

It sounded like a nursery rhyme to Anthea who had no voice left. The air was thick and stifling. She felt as if she was trying to breathe cotton wool. Between the trees she saw the island, floating calmly, waiting for them—riding on the surface of a sea reflecting both sunset and an approaching storm. She stopped. Griff took her hand coaxingly.

"Come on!" he said softly. "It's a pity to stop when you are so close."

"Do we—have to *swim?*" she asked.

"Oh, no! Don't be silly! There's always a boat," said Griff.

They came out of the woodland along the track which was clear for the last few yards. The edges were cut and neatened as if someone had been working on it only that afternoon. There was a spade stuck in the ground and a peaked cap hung on the spade. Then the road ended forever. There was no sign of the road mender anywhere. Only his spade and cap on the edge of the lonely shore. They stepped off the road onto the beach and stared out over the glassy water before them.

The surface was not completely smooth. Little ripples roughened it from time to time, although Anthea could feel no wind. At some points the woods came down almost to the water's edge. Further out, its reflection was so clear that there was no telling the island from its image, except that one was upside down.

"There," said Griff, pointing. Drawn up on the bank under one of the trees was a little boat, its oars neatly shipped and laid inside it. The strip of sand was narrow just there. The trees hung directly over the boat and dropped leaves into it.

"Can you row?" Anthea asked.

There was an odd vibration underfoot, as if somewhere, on another shore, waves were pounding the sand so furiously that they could feel it here, where the water was completely calm. Two dragonish islands floated breast to breast. Yet there was still that rhythmical beat coming up through the sand. Griff felt it, too.

"Hurry," he ordered, pulling her toward the boat. But he had to untwist his fingers from hers to get the boat into the water. Anthea was forced to bend and push and straighten with him.

There, on the sand, as she bent toward it, Anthea saw a strange shadow. It was very faint—but it was a shadow she had seen before. She strained away from Griff, looking behind her.

Between the trees, half-hidden by tall grasses, was a statue, the head and shoulders of a woman looking down at them through a veil that was loosely knotted under her chin. This statue was not as immaculate as the one in the hall had been at the very beginning of Anthea's journey. It was weathered and worn, slightly tilted to one side and blackened with lichen.

"Look," Anthea panted. "Here it is again, but worn out."

"Look!" said Griff at the same time. The slight tremble in the ground had grown stronger. There was a sound in the air. Along the edge of the lake a dark cloud was moving toward them. The storm had come to earth and was threatening to ride them down.

"Horses," said Griff. "Come on!" He grabbed her arm above the elbow. "Get into the boat! I'll push off."

Anthea stared at the approaching herd. Horses! And on the first horse rode a woman warrior, waving and crying out to her. Anthea could hear her words though she was still some distance away, though the hoofs thundered like a real storm.

"Anthea! Don't go! You don't have to!"

"Come on!" cried Griff, jerking at the chain. Anthea took a deep, struggling breath and stood straighter.

"No," she said. "I don't have to."

It was as if she had spoken a spell. She felt entirely free. The wall dissolved. Air rushed easily into her lungs. The stretched chain snapped, and the little padlock swung down under Anthea's wrist like a pendulum.

"You do have to! I *have* to have company," Griff cried, then stopped as if he was not quite sure of what he was saying.

"No, you don't," Anthea said. "You've got this far. Go on your own."

"Go on my own!" exclaimed Griff, outraged. "Go on my own!" he repeated, as if he was seriously thinking about it.

"It's *your* adventure! Not mine!" Anthea said. "Not anymore."

But the horses were on them. Griff leaped into the boat and pushed himself out a little way. Anthea scrambled up between the trees and clung to the statue. The horses streamed below her, and Anthea saw the gray veil over the statue's hidden face move a little in the wind of the passage. It was no longer stone. It was nothing but a sheet of cobwebs.

The horses swept by, churning the shallow sea to foam. They neighed. They tossed their heads. Then they were gone. The chain dangled from her wrist, and out at sea, Griff rocked in his boat, staring in astonishment. Beside her she could see the face of the statue. It was smiling under its cobwebs, not crying. Its tears were used up. Its grief was gone. It was trying out a new expression. Anthea smiled, too. Then someone, not Griff, said her name, and she turned around, startled. It was the woman warrior. It was Flora.

Anthea, though she had rescued herself, recognized a rescuer, and could have wept with relief and happiness. She was forgiven for the things she had said, and more than that. Whatever fights they had had and might have, she and Flora were tied together, not only by blood, but by all sorts of hidden admiration. They would never desert one another. Beside Flora, on another horse, rode a half-naked boy Anthea vaguely recognized.

Griff stood up in his boat.

"Leo," he shouted. "Leo!" His face was bright, this time with simple pleasure. He had become a brother, not a demon: "I've been waiting for ages. I was just going to set out alone."

"I'm sorry," said Leo, sliding off his horse. "I was held up."

"Look how far I got, though," cried Griff, shoving his oars clumsily into the shallow water and beginning to row the boat back toward the beach.

"I'm sorry," Flora called up to Anthea. "I do want you to live with us, really. Come back home. We'll ask Molly if you can have one of the Gelerts all for yourself."

It was easier to say such things in Viridian than it was to say them in real life—and once they were said, they were understood in both places.

"I was going to anyway," said Anthea. "To come home, I mean."

"I don't really want you to go away," Flora said. "It's just . . . you know!"

She, too, climbed off her horse.

"Look," said Anthea, pointing at the statue. "The veil's gone. She can see. She looks like someone I know."

Flora looked up at it without much interest.

"She looks just like you," she said. Then she turned back to the boys, now both together in the boat.

"You can row," Griff was saying. "I'm out of practice."

"*You* can row," Leo was saying. "This is *your* space. You can take me the rest of the way."

"It's a long way," Anthea said, looking out at the island.

"We've come a long way already," Griff pointed out. "It's not far, really. Not with company."

One of those strange shivers ran over the surface of the sea, and thousands of little crests of water caught the light. As far as the eye could see the ocean shimmered.

"We'll never know if you've arrived safely," Anthea said. She was sure they would arrive safely, yet at the same time she wanted to see how this other strange story finished, so closely linked by many chains to her own.

"We'll light a fire on the beach when we get there," said Leo, leaning over the back of the boat. Ripple after ripple swelled and spread gracefully behind them. "You never know. Look after my house, won't you?"

"If . . . if you see anyone swimming there, on the island I mean, give them my love," Anthea called.

But Griff was dipping the oars again, and the ripples ran out in a series of widening circles, overlapped, and were lost. The boat moved away.

"Anthea," called Griff out of the growing darkness. "Thanks! Thanks for coming so far."

"Thank *you*, Flora," called Leo, perhaps a little mockingly.

The girls waved but made no reply. The boat went on and on until it was entirely swallowed by darkness. Sitting on the sand, Flora leaned against Anthea, Anthea against Flora.

"I never really meant any of those things I said," Flora explained again.

"Nor did I," said Anthea. "Not really. We'll never ever quarrel ever again."

"Just sometimes, to stay in practice," said Flora, and they smiled together in the dark, waiting for someone to light a fire on the distant beach. The waves washed on the sand saying "Hush! Hush!" and all Viridian hushed in the darkness. It was hardly surprising that Flora's eyes closed, or that Anthea went to sleep.

They woke at the same second, staring at each other through the hole in the wall. It was raining. There was no thunder or lightning, just a simple homely drumming. They didn't say a word. There seemed to be nothing left to say. There were footsteps in the hall. Molly banged, first on one door and then on the other.

"Good news!" she said. "There's been a landslide up the

hill, the school bus can't get through, and Lionel can't get out."

As she spoke someone began hammering out in the big room.

Flora sat up. "Terrific! No school today!" she said. "Good luck, at last!"

Chapter 17

IT RAINED ALL DAY.

"A thousand curses," said Flora. "A day off school and we're shut in the house with all this hammering."

"Everyone *wanted* him to hammer yesterday," Anthea pointed out.

To her surprise she was almost sorry to see a corner of the skeleton house vanishing under a new skin. She would never forget that, under painted surfaces, houses had their own secret spaces filled with wiring and pipes and insulation, or that everything was secretly connected even if people did not want to look closely at the connections.

"We've never had such a successful fight before," Molly said. She looked almost curiously at Lionel, who smiled back absentmindedly and perhaps rather sadly, looking from top to bottom of a new wall, successfully begun and successfully finished, as rain streamed down the window.

"I'm hammering my old man out," he said, "and I'm probably hammering myself in."

"Old Lionel's gone already," Flora cried triumphantly. "Otherwise you'd still be having breakfast and complaining about the Minister of Finance."

"I'll be the next ghost of the house perhaps," Lionel suggested, rubbing a nail hole with his thumb. "Where's the plastic wood?"

"As if I'd let you!" Molly said, rattling through the bead curtain. "Here it is!"

"The rain will be good for the new forest," Anthea said.

"Good for us, too," Flora said. "Go out on the verandah and listen to the water tank filling. We'll be able to have a shower each."

So Anthea went out and listened to the rain rushing along the guttering at the edge of the verandah roof, toppling through the downpipe into the water tank and, somewhere along the way, turning from sky water into house water. A gossipy ripple ran around the eaves, telling the lives of people and ghosts, one tale running into another without a moment's pause. Anthea had believed she was resigned at last to the crowded house, but she was still pleased to sit by herself at the rickety table, staring seriously out over the soft gray-green countryside.

Something had altered, but what was it? *She* had changed, but had the house really changed too? Had the ghosts of those long-ago boys moved on at last, or was it simply that she was set free from her own ghosts . . . those golden merpeople, laughing and sunbathing on their little, lost island. For they were certainly gone, gone with Leo and Griff, leaving her behind, alive and free, to watch gentle veils of rain sweeping in across the harbor and to listen to the active melody of water in the guttering. She remembered how Viridian had trickled and flowed as she came down beside the snowline, and smiled to herself, thinking that she had melted in her own way, and that her house (*her* house now, as much as Flora's) was contained by an even larger house—huge and invisible, but *there*. The house sheltered the family, but the family held the idea of the house, the family with its own wiring and connections hidden from everyday view beneath the family skin. Yesterday, she had fought with Flora, but that particular fight was over forever. There would be new fights, of course, because two such different people were bound to argue, but she would always remember Flora riding the wild horse along the beach, shouting her name as she came, shouting, "Anthea! Anthea! Don't go!"

As Anthea remembered this, Flora herself came staggering out, weighed down on one side by the pig bucket. Her yellow raincoat was draped across her shoulders and she looked like a road-mender's tent on legs. Glancing meaningfully at Anthea, she sighed noisily. Anthea knew what that sigh meant, and this morning at least, she did not mind.

"I'll take half the handle," she offered amiably.

"Jack and Jill went down the hill," chanted Flora, making room for her to share the handle. "To take a pail of pig-food."

"The fat from ham," said Anthea looking sideways into the bucket.

"The old plum jam," added Flora.

"The beans-that-grew-too-big food."

Anthea laughed, turned up her face to the sky. The rain trickled down her cheeks and around each side of her nose. She licked the drops away.

"This is what trees feel," she cried, as they passed the forest. "Lovely water running down over them, and then soaking into them."

"It's soaking into you," Flora pointed out.

"I'm being irrigated," Anthea agreed. "Hey, Flora?"

"Yes?"

"You know that place I—we—dreamed about . . . Viridian . . . Do you think it's still there, in the stereoscope? Locked in?"

Without consulting each other they put the pig bucket down and wriggled their fingers, for the thin handle had cut into them.

"It was a game they played, dead Henry and Leo . . . old Lionel, that is . . ." Flora began. "Henry made a country out of the pictures and the stereoscope space, because Lionel was the oldest and took up all the house room. Henry died young and Lionel died old, but I suppose they both stayed around in the spaces they liked best, using the names they'd chosen for themselves."

"They kept on missing each other," Anthea suggested. "They needed each other to get to the island."

"They needed *us*," Flora replied, with the satisfaction of someone who has taken things over and put them right. "Without us, they'd still be wasting time in hyperspace or whatever it was. And now the house isn't haunted anymore. It's funny about space. You have to have it, but you can't just stay in it forever. You have to make way or there's nowhere for anyone else to go."

They picked up the bucket and plodded on, leaning slightly outward against its inward tug. But Anthea couldn't help wondering if the long-ago brothers were still the true ghosts of the house. "Let's hope it rains all weekend," said Flora. "Now that Lionel's really working on the walls, I mean."

She wondered about the sad time in old Lionel's life when he had worked on the house, pushing out its verandah and adding rooms. Nobody had ever suggested he was very sad. Perhaps it had been a secret sadness, told only to wood and tin, running down his arm and through his hammer and into the nails. If the house had known, well, it was being changed and would soon forget. No one would remember old Lionel's sadness.

Toward evening the rain lessened and stopped. Almost, it seemed, in a matter of seconds, the clouds broke apart, the sun came out, and the world glittered in every direction.

"A scrap dinner tonight," Molly said, for the table was covered with lengths of wood and Lionel's retractable tape measure, and his square and level and saw—all tools of the home builder. "Everything's in a worse mess than usual."

"You *asked* for it," Lionel pointed out.

"I'm not complaining," Molly replied. "But how about scrambled eggs? I've just been around the nests."

"Great!" said Lionel. "It's time that pack of feathered bandits did something for their keep . . . apart from defiling the verandah, that is."

"Well," Molly remarked, "when you've finished putting the lining on the walls you might like to build a henhouse."

Lionel looked at her, narrowing his eyes in a sinister fashion, feeling the edge of the chisel.

"Who knows what I might do!" was all he said.

"We'd better not kill the rooster, because *he* might begin haunting. He's another one who thinks he owns the place," Flora declared, and she and Anthea laughed, though the thought of a ghostly rooster running out of the grass at early morning legs was more alarming than the thought of most ghosts.

Flora and Anthea spread out a rug on the floor. There was something strange and pleasant about picnicking on the floor of your own house, about setting out plates and knives and forks on the floor. Zeppelin and both cats looked through the glass doors. But Zeppelin soon went back to the Gelerts in their box in the laundry. One of them was fated to stay to be Anthea's own private dog, provided she promised to mop up the puddles it would no doubt make around the house until it learned better manners. The hens wandered backward and forward, peering in and tapping at the glass with their beaks, even though they had been given plenty of mash to supplement what they scratched up for themselves.

"Don't let them see the eggshells, though," Flora said.

"It might make them go all funny. They might want *vengeance*."

"Family wiped out by the revenge of killer hens," Anthea added.

"We'd never survive," Lionel said. "Now, before the walls were lined, we could have just climbed straight up them and hidden next to the ceiling . . ."

All the things that had been set out along the joists were now lined up on the floor.

"Where will we put it all?" Molly asked.

"Sort it through, and throw it out," Lionel advised. "Hang on to the false teeth, though. We'll need them someday when we're old."

Anthea left the room, and then came rather shyly through the bead curtain into the kitchen. Flora was stirring the scrambled eggs. Molly was setting out a carton of honey, a jar of plum jam, and another of peanut butter on a tray.

"Molly," said Anthea a little breathlessly, "I know it's only a picnic, but we could—we could decorate it." She held out her honey pot with the silver bee on it, still partly wrapped in the last piece of tissue paper. Flora's mouth fell open.

"Anthea!" Molly said, with a smile and a sigh. "It's too nice. Put it away again."

Flora's mouth snapped shut.

"Put the plum jam in it," she said quickly. "I'll eat plum jam if comes out of that pot."

"It's a *honey* pot," Molly said. "Look at the bee."

"Suppose it's really a wasp," Flora cried. "Wasps like jam."

Everything changes, thought Anthea in astonishment. Somehow she knew that, even when she was grown-up and in another house, maybe with children of her own, she would always think of the pot as having a silver wasp on it. "What a pretty pot," people would say. "I love the bee on it." And she, and possibly her children too, would cry, "It's a wasp!"

"Even Lionel will eat the jam from a wasp pot like this," Flora said.

The big room smelled of new wood. The pale half-lined walls looked as if they were refusing to associate with the unlined ones. It was like being in a past room and a future one at the same time. The picnic was a great success. Teddy in particular loved the new jam pot.

"Bzzzz!" he said, pointing to it, then snatching his finger away, shrieking at his own courage.

As it darkened outside, the hens went to roost on Molly's car, and Flora and Anthea, having been forced to help with the dishes, wandered out into the evening. They didn't plan to go anywhere particular, but one way and another, partly arguing, partly joking, they walked out along the peninsula, Wakefield's Point or Old Daisy.

Though the sun had set, a rim of light lingered around the hill behind them, reflected out by the mouth of the harbor. The island looked closer and blacker than usual. Suddenly Flora caught Anthea's arm.

"Look!" she cried. "A fire."

Someone had indeed lit a little fire on the beach of the island. They could see the flames leaping up and, black against the flames, figures running backward and forward piling on more driftwood.

"Is it them?" asked Anthea. "Is it a sign?"

"There's more than two of them," Flora said, peering out toward the island at the figures, dancing in and out of the distant glow. "I wish we were there."

"Oh, well," said Anthea. "If Lionel mends the boat we might go there one day. We'll light our own fire and find our own driftwood." ·

"We'll do our own dance," Flora agreed. "Well, we're beginning it now, really. A sort of slow dance."

The sun went down. The light on the hills died, and the fire burned, leaping wildly up at the dark. Anthea turned around and looked down at the steady lights in the house behind them.

"We'd better go home," she said. "Molly said she'd read us a story."

"A ghost story," said Flora, making ghost eyes and flinging up her hands.

"Been there, done that," said Anthea. "I want wild horses and beautiful barbarian chieftainesses. . . . Though, come to think of it, I've done that, too. When you came riding along the beach in Viridian, you looked like a beautiful chieftainess."

"Really?" cried Flora, and she felt herself loving Anthea, who had not only seen her as she knew herself to be, but had lived to describe it. Greedily, she wanted to ask Anthea for more detail, but all she said was, "How about something totally different . . . a funny story!"

"A funny one would be great," agreed Anthea. "I suppose if you don't keep laughing, you get out of practice."

So they went home, side by side this time, picking their way over the peninsula, which seemed to sigh around them as if either the evening or the land were breathing contentedly. Behind them, across the dark, murmuring sea, the fire and its reflection died down to nothing. The shapes—the dancing ghosts that had moved around it—became part of the good darkness, and the whole island vanished at last, an indistinguishable part of the night.